Freedom Bound

Donna Campbell

Copyright © 2018 Donna Campbell

All rights reserved.

ISBN:1986985326
ISBN-13: 978-1986985321

DEDICATION

This one is for all the ones who want to be free, but need a little help finding the way to the door.

Cover Design by David Campbell

Edited by James Barringer

Published by DC Books, Ocoee, FL

ACKNOWLEDGMENTS

Thank you Lani, Angie, and Rachael for reading this while I was still writing it and giving me such great suggestions when I needed help. Thank you for helping to bring the Copeland Family and all those they come in contact with to life. Y'all are superdeeduper.

Part One

1

The hot sun pressed down on Oliver, making each arduous step more difficult than the last as he lumbered along the marked hiking path of the nature reserve. Dirt mixed with sweat and clung to every inch of exposed skin. Perspiration trickled down his neck and waist ensuring that the filth would coat his entire body. Nevertheless, he tried to enjoy himself. Trees rose high above his head, while a myriad of plants, bushes, and flowers covered the ground on either side of the trail. Birdsong rang out from the trees. Butterflies flitted from flower to flower, accompanied by a wide variety of bugs. He swatted at a fly that seemed intent on landing on him.

Not wanting to draw attention to himself, he tried to curtail his limp and hide the pain he felt in his left leg. Deborah and Ash walked ahead of him, holding hands and laughing often as they talked. Deborah had once been his mother's assistant, but had quickly become a friend and now a member of the family, along with her husband Ash. Ash carried a pack filled with family essentials on his back and toted his son Daniel in a baby carrier on his chest. As far as Oliver could tell, Ash had not even broken a sweat. Three-year-old Asha walked next to Oliver, holding his hand and stopping frequently to pick up a stick, a leaf, or a bug. The sprightly girl took delight in getting as dirty as possible on the hike, and, Oliver noted, in any situation possible.

Hiking had never been one of Oliver's preferred activities. Dirt and insects, and the rocks which continually tried to trip him, were not among favorite his things. Not only did he like cleanliness and order, he needed cleanliness and order in his life. But he loved Deborah and Asher so he had said yes when they had invited him on the hike. In addition to enjoying time with the Levines, Oliver desperately wanted to regain some of his old strength and get back to the athletic and capable man he had once been. He had been on his college crew and polo teams. He had spent weekends on the tennis courts or in the swimming pool. He had spent winters skiing and summers yachting. He had been a scholar with a genius IQ; spoke Spanish, French, and Portuguese fluently; and could decipher just about any Latin-based language easily.

But that was before the skiing accident had nearly killed him. After his broken bones had mended, he was left with a brain injury which gave him left-sided weakness, memory problems, and difficulty controlling his emotions. There was no way Oliver planned to give in to the label of disabled; he hated to think of himself that way and despised the idea that other people probably did think of him as, if not fully disabled, at least incapacitated. He was determined to hide any limitations and become the robust and powerful man he had once been. But even this supposed easy family hike was wiping him out.

A tug on his hand pulled Oliver from his reverie. "Honey! Honey!" Asha was pulling his hand, trying to loose her own from his grip.

He looked down into Asha's big pleading brown eyes and couldn't help but smile. "Yes, Sweetie?" He loved that she called him Honey. Honey had been her pet name for him for as long as either of them could remember.

The moniker had originated when the toddler heard Oliver's mother Catherine call him honey and decided that was his name.

"Look!" She pointed to his left to show him a large spider web with a very large brown and red spider in its center. "Oh! It's so pretty!" She continued to tug, trying to rush over and take a closer look at the creature.

Oliver shivered and tightened his grip. How could she be so unafraid of anything? He swallowed his own fear, smiled and said, "Yes, it is pretty. Let's let him finish his morning nap, shall we?"

"Yes, Honey," Asha said dejectedly.

He hated saying no to her and decided he would buy her a toy later to make up for it.

Ash and Deborah had stopped ahead of them, perhaps to see if Oliver would allow their daughter to touch the spider. No, he reminded himself, they knew him better than that and they trusted him. It was more likely they were letting him and Asha catch up so the slower pair would not fall too far behind. Deborah was rifling through the backpack Ash wore. She pulled out two water bottles and handed one to Oliver. After taking a long swig from hers, she gave some to Asha and then handed the bottle to Ash. "There is a place just around the bend with a bench. I thought we could eat lunch and decide if we want to take the blue or green trail." She looked at Oliver and he thought he saw alarm in her eyes for a moment. "I think," she said, "the green trail will be easier for Asha."

Do I really look that bad? He knew he felt tired but wondered if it showed so much. Or maybe he had imagined the alarm on Deborah's face. Regardless, he was fine taking the easier and shorter trail and relieved to have a rest for lunch. "Steady on to the bench, then," he said with all the cheerfulness and energy he could muster. Oliver drank the cool water, appreciating that Deborah had known he wouldn't like drinking from the same bottle as anyone else.

The family arrived at the bench, and Asher unpacked food while Deborah spread a blanket on the ground for the children. She took her sleeping son from the carrier and held him for a minute before laying him on the soft clean blanket.

Asha was about to plop herself down next to her brother when Ash said, "Oh no you don't, young lady. How do you get so dirty just taking a walk?" He pulled wipes from the pack and handed them to Oliver. "Uncle Oliver will clean you up first; then you may sit down and eat your lunch."

As Oliver wiped the dirt off her, Asha closed her eyes. "Why do you have your eyes closed?" he asked. "I've already washed your face."

"Oh, Honey, there's so much stuff that wants me to pick it up that I have to 'nore it and not see it." She squeezed her eyes tighter for emphasis. "I'm hungry as a horse and I could eat a bear!"

Asha loved that phrase, so Oliver answered the same way he always did. "What kind of bear could you eat? Black bears are too mean and brown bears are too big." The in-joke had started when he had accidentally said "hungry as a horse" several months earlier, and Ash had added the "eat a bear" part. Asha, always sharp, had wondered aloud what sort of bear a person could eat. She had laughed for several minutes at Oliver's retort, though she couldn't have understood why it was funny.

"A blue beary, a straw beary, or even a razz beary!" Asha giggled and opened her eyes. "Honey, are you done yet? I want my samwich, please."

He looked at her and supposed baby wipes could only do so much. "Yes; go eat." He took the five blackened wipes over to the trash can, grabbed a clean one for himself, and washed his face and hands before joining the family for lunch. It was a small thing, but it made him feel no cleaner. He felt that the dirt had ground itself into his skin and bore its way into every pore.

After they finished eating, Ash and Oliver talked about soccer while they cleaned up and repacked and Asha picked wildflowers just off the trail as Deborah fed the baby. Oliver hoisted the backpack, trying to work out how to get the straps around his shoulders. "I'll carry the backpack. It's my turn."

"No," Asher said, taking it and putting it on in one easy motion. "I've got it. It's full of Daniel and Asha's things. You shouldn't have to carry it." He then put the baby carrier on and let Deborah put Daniel in it for him.

Oliver felt humiliation form and turn to indignation. He was not an invalid, and he was more than capable of carrying the backpack. It seemed everyone thought he was weak. He wanted to yell like a teenager, stomp his foot and demand he be treated with respect. Rather than say anything, though, he pushed his reaction down and gave a very convincing but insincere smile, a skill he had perfected on his mother. "Alright," he said looking at the fork in the trail. One was marked with a green post and the other a blue post. "Which way shall we go?"

After a beat Deborah said, "Let's take the green trail. I think Asha might be getting tired and I want to get her to the car before her nap time."

Had they already discussed which path to take? Perhaps they had. Oliver was certain now they must have talked about it, but he didn't remember. He took Asha's little hand in his and followed Deborah and Asher down the trail toward the car park. "I can do all things through Him that strengthens me," he murmured quietly.

At home that afternoon Oliver took a long, hot shower to wash the grime and sweat off. The steam of the shower worked to relax his stiff muscles. He was reminded of his life before the accident that had taken away his athleticism. In a strange way, he missed being sore and exhausted, or at least he missed being exhausted from playing outside instead of from climbing the stairs. Everything wore him out these days: reading, going to work, taking simple four-mile walks in the woods. But he didn't want to keep dwelling on who he used to be or continue feeling that his current self wasn't good enough. He let the hot water take his negative feelings and wash them down the drain.

There was a knock on his bedroom door. "Daddy!" he heard Sarah calling.

He turned off the shower, stepped out, put his robe on and grabbed a towel for his hair. "Just a moment." Rubbing his hair with the towel he walked to the bedroom door and opened it to see his impatient fifteen-year-old daughter tapping her foot.

"Daddy, I'm sorry I interrupted your shower, but I need an answer now. I have to answer Tommy right now. You were taking so long." She looked every bit like her mother. She had the same shade of blonde hair that his ex-wife had, the same nose and the same chin, but she had his hazel eyes.

"What is the question you need answered?"

Sarah released an exasperated sigh. "Tommy wants to know if he can take me to dinner and then the movies tonight. Daddy, please say yes." She stood on her tip toes and kissed his cheek.

"He'll need to come in and let me meet him." Oliver checked the time. It was just after three, far too early to dress for dinner. He sat down on his bed and considered a nap.

"Daddy, you met Tommy already, and

besides, he wants me to meet him and the rest of the gang at the restaurant. Please, Daddy." She went to his dresser and began taking clothes out for him. He knew she loved choosing his clothes. "I really like him and you said you thought he was a gentleman. You talked about rowing with him." She took a comb and began combing her father's light brown wavy hair.

His daughter was pulling out all the stops, and Oliver smiled slightly. He would let the persuasion work. "Tommy will come here and pick you up, or you will not go. What movie is he taking you to see?" Oliver took the comb from Sarah and combed his hair quickly into the style he preferred.

Sarah seemed to know her father had met her halfway. "Thank you, Daddy!" She kissed his cheek again and hugged him. "He wants to see the new comedy, the one with bank robbery gone wrong. It's PG-13, Daddy." Sarah knew all the questions her father would ask before he asked them. "It starts at 8:00 at the Belleshore Cineplex. There are four other kids going. I have my cell."

"Okay. He will come inside when he picks you up, and you will be home by 11:00." Oliver met his daughter's eyes. "And he will not come inside when he brings you home."

"Thank you again, Daddy!" Sarah sang as she skipped from the room.

Oliver picked up his phone and made a memo about Tommy and the rules he had given his daughter, who, sweet though she was, sometimes tried to take advantage of his less than perfect memory.

2

Catherine Copeland was tired. She couldn't remember when she had been so tired before. The doorbell rang downstairs, prompting her to check her dress and makeup in the mirror before going down to meet her dinner guests. Hosting dinners, parties, and other events was one of the things she had always enjoyed doing but tonight she wished she could have canceled. There was no reason to be so drained, but drained was what she felt.

Straightening her back and holding her head high, she entered the sitting room of Cumberland Manor, the palatial estate she shared with Oliver and Sarah. Ian, the butler who had been with the family for more than two decades, was serving drinks to the

Sumners. Oliver sat in the corner talking with Phyllis Sumner's niece; he stood when his mother entered.

What was that girl's name? Well, whatever her name, she wasn't a girl anymore; she was in her thirties and had never married. Catherine was certain that Gordon and Phyllis Sumner had invited her to dinner in the hope of marrying their niece off to Oliver. Her son looked at her as if he longed to be rescued from the plump, pretty woman, but Catherine merely nodded at him as she glided over to Phyllis and Gordon.

Glad to let Phyllis do most of the talking, Catherine found a seat and let Phyllis and Gordon follow her over to the settee as Phyllis continued telling her about how wonderful her niece Vera was and what an accomplished professor she had become. Vera! Yes, that was the girl's name. She taught art history at some university. Catherine was having a difficult time concentrating on the conversation; she longed to slip into bed and sleep. Why should she be so tired?

Ian rang the dinner bell and the group walked into the dining room. Oliver sat down next to Gordon and Vera seated herself on his other side. It was clear to Catherine that he had hoped to escape her. She had no plans to rescue her son. It would do him good to get out, date a little, and eventually find a new wife. Vera was suitable for him. She was intelligent, had plenty of her own money, and enjoyed society life enough to keep Oliver involved and take that burden away from her. She knew he didn't care about the galas, fundraisers, or other events. It was a chore getting him to go to anything other than the philharmonic. As such, she had every intention of making him talk to Vera for the evening. "Gordon, how's the new yacht? I heard you hired a new captain. Is that right?"

"Yes, a chap named Martin Tripp, came highly recommended. I skipper the boat recreationally, but I hired Martin for the regattas. We're considering wintering in Panama this year. You haven't seen the new yacht yet, have you? She's called *Freedom's Joy*, and she's a beauty, fifty-two feet and three cabins. You will have to come aboard. In fact, what about lunch on Saturday? Invite Simon, Denise, and of course," he turned to Oliver. "Oliver, you must come. And bring Sarah if she isn't already busy."

Catherine waited for Oliver to answer. She could see him moving his mind from whatever conversation he and Vera had been having to consider Gordon's request. She knew the effort this was for her son; multiple conversations and multiple subjects within one conversation were difficult for him. If her often reticent son didn't answer, she was ready to speak for him. After about fifteen seconds, he did answer.

"Thank you, Mr. Sumner. I would be honored. I believe my daughter already has plans. I think she mentioned a pool party with some school friends."

"Uncle Gordon," Vera said, "I hope I won't be too forward if I invite myself."

"Vera, darling, you are always invited," Phyllis answered with a knowing smile.

"I'll invite Simon and Denise in the morning, but you know Simon loves yachts, and I am certain he has been waiting for an invitation to inspect *Freedom's Joy*." Catherine hoped Simon would come. In fact, she wished he were here this evening. Her charming son would have taken some of the hosting burden off her when she was feeling so weary. Oliver was just not the extrovert her younger son was. She had a bit of pity on him as she watched him squirm under Vera's attentions. The girl was a bit forward, almost brazen, wasn't she?

Catherine finally decided to rescue Oliver from the claws Vera was trying to put into him. "Oliver, how are plans for Sarah's Sweet Sixteen coming?"

He breathed an audible sigh of relief and turned towards her. "Oh, Sarah is thrilled with how it's coming along. I believe she has invited the entire sophomore class. She has two outfits and is trying to talk me into a third one. I wonder if her wedding will cost me as much, but of course I don't mind. She is my little princess after all."

The talk turned towards Sweet Sixteen parties and how quickly the charming little girl was growing up. Catherine sat back in her seat, relieved that didn't have to keep the conversation moving. Phyllis, despite never having children of her own, bragged about her supposedly perfect nieces and nephews as if they were her own. She loved to talk and managed to bring up each of them in the conversation in response to how well Sarah was doing in school and in her various efforts.

As the conversation continued, Catherine watched her son as he kept quiet and let Phyllis talk. Her heart ached for him at times. Although it was not evident to anybody else, she could see the remnants of the skiing accident in his life. She saw the deliberation it took for him to maintain a conversation. She noticed the grimaces from the pain left over from the broken bones and atrophied muscles. The defensiveness he tried not to express showed in his eyes, and only Catherine caught it. The self-control he had mastered over his fragile emotions, and the fear over someone realizing he had forgotten something, were hidden from everyone but her. She knew him better than anybody in the world. She saw what others didn't. They saw an intelligent soft-spoken gentleman; she saw a man struggling to maintain that face to them. People who met him would never guess what he had gone through and what he still went through.

At times she saw him as he was when he was brought to the hospital, swollen, bruised and comatose, unrecognizable to anyone but her. When she noticed his determination to find a word or saw his trepidation before walking down a flight of stairs, she remembered how utterly pitiful he had looked when he first woke from the coma, unable to speak, unable to tell anyone his needs. But she had been there by his side, and she had known what he wanted to say. She had understood him before anyone else. As his speech had returned, his bones mended, and he learned to walk again, she could not have been more proud of him. He had a strength even he was unaware of, a strength that most people never saw behind his apparent frailty. But Catherine saw it. It only made her want to protect him even more. He might never know how difficult it had been for her to stand back and watch him struggle and sometimes fall, but she hoped he knew how much she loved him and how very proud she was of him.

After dessert had been eaten and the Sumners had gone home, Catherine was more than ready for bed. Though she knew how much Oliver hated to play cards, he offered to play gin rummy with her. On any other night she would have taken him up on the offer, but on this occasion she said no, kissed his cheek, and gratefully went upstairs to the sleep that called out to her.

3

The Prestige Men's Club was a throwback to the exclusive businessmen's clubs of the fifties and sixties. Cigar smoke hung in the air, well-dressed men gathered, and the only women in sight served drinks. Oliver entered and scanned the crowd for Simon. He found his brother sitting in a red leather wingback chair and reading a newspaper. Simon had belonged to Belle Cay's business networking organization for several years, and had insisted that Oliver, as the CEO of Copeland Enterprises, needed to be a member as well. Oliver wasn't so sure; so far, he had discussed very little business and had more often spoken to other businessmen about the things they did when they weren't at work. To Oliver it was just a place where men could get together to smoke cigars, drink scotch, and feel important. Simon assured him that these connections could and would work out for his benefit and the benefit of the company overall.

Simon looked up and waved Oliver over to sit in the matching wingback next to his. "Ollie! So good to see you! I feel as if I'm always so busy with the kids and the foundation that I hardly see you anymore."

"We see each other at least twice a week," said Oliver, thinking of family dinners, church, and the regularly occurring galas.

"I mean when it can be just the two of us, Big Brother, and we can really talk." Simon stood and hugged his obviously uncomfortable brother. "Oliver, it took us too long to find out we were friends, and I don't want us to ever forget it."

The two sat down just as an attractive woman appeared, dressed in a professional and slightly provocative black and white waitress' uniform. "How are you?" she asked, without waiting for an answer. It seemed to Oliver people never really wanted an answer to that question. "Welcome to Prestige. May I get you something to eat or drink?"

"Yes, lemonade, please." Oliver told her.

He watched her walk away before turning back to Simon. "So, how are you? Is everything well?"

Simon sat back in his chair and gave a satisfied smile. "Things are well. The twins are as rambunctious as ever and starting kindergarten in the fall. Mother says God is paying me back double for the trouble I caused as a kid. Jackson talked Kyle into hiding from Maggie, the nanny, for about three hours yesterday. Poor thing was frantic when she couldn't find them. Misha is excited about starting pre-kindergarten. He already has his first day's clothes picked out and the first day is how far off?. And Cathy is enjoying being spoiled. She can speak in full sentences, but around her brothers she always seems to use baby talk. Denise is thinking of going back to work, maybe in private practice. I have quite the full life. I couldn't be happier."

Oliver admired his gregarious brother, who he never would have imagined as such a good husband and father. Yet he was. His children were doted upon and encouraged to be resilient, creative, and independent. Simon cherished Denise without smothering her. There was a time when Oliver had been certain that the only person who mattered to

Simon was Simon, but now as he watched him be a father and husband, he knew he had misjudged his brother.

"Will you be coming aboard Gordon Sumner's cruiser this weekend? I think he might take her out on the water," said Simon. "In fact, I think he's turned it into a full-fledged party."

"Yes, it should be nice. I have to admit I'm relieved you're coming because he's been sicking Vera on me lately and she is clearly interested in snagging me." Oliver made his hands into claws and pantomimed them grasping him and choking him. He shuddered at the thought. The woman was nice enough, but she talked non-stop about herself; worse, she was brash, and her sense of humor was anything but lady-like.

Simon laughed "If her message is that clear to you, my brother, then she must be coming on strong indeed. I'll ask Denise to keep her off you. Vera likes her because Denise lets her talk about herself and all her latest undertakings. In fact, I heard Vera is being asked to curate at the art museum."

"What do you mean if it's clear to me?" Oliver tried to hide his hurt over the presumed insult.

Simon leaned forward and put his hand

on Oliver's arm, assuring him there was no insult intended. "Women are practically falling over themselves to get you to notice them. You're the subject of many conversations amongst the women of Belle Cay, Ollie. They say you're Belle Cay's most eligible bachelor, and you are oblivious to all of it. And your obliviousness apparently makes you all the more desirable. Ollie, buddy, you could be quite the ladies' man if you chose to be."

Even though Simon seemed very serious, Oliver couldn't bring himself to believe what his brother was saying; he had never noticed a single woman besides Vera show interest in him. "Really?" Oliver asked in astonishment. He imagined himself trying to juggle multiple women and ineptly forgetting their names, or worse yet calling one by another's name. "Really? Well, I don't want to be a ladies' man, and I wouldn't know how. I think I'll stick to just taking care of my Sarah."

A tall, fit man with dark brown hair approached the brothers, fixing his gaze on Oliver. "Excuse me, you are Mr. Copeland, aren't you?"

Wondering what the man could possibly want, Oliver looked at him for several seconds before answering. "Yes, I'm Oliver Copeland."

What kind of gentleman would not introduce himself before asking for a stranger's name? Simon quickly interjected, "I'm Simon Copeland. And you are…?" He held his hand out to the man but didn't offer him a seat yet.

"Ah, yes forgive me. My name is Nathan Westley." He was young, yet spoke with the confidence of a much older man. "I just finished my MBA at Yale." He again turned to Oliver. "You are a legend there. Summa cum laude, captain of the rowing team that went to the world championships in your senior year, and now the CEO of a Fortune 500 company. I was summering in Belle Cay, but decided I had to make my permanent home here. Well, anyway, I saw your picture in the paper, in the story about the new wing of the medical center, and I had to take the opportunity to meet you."

Nathan Westley had spoken so quickly that Oliver was still processing his words. He sat looking at the man, quietly surprised at having his résumé repeated back to him in the form of such lavish flattery, and said nothing. He was reminded of the fans that Ash sometimes encountered when they were out together. Ash played bass in the rock band Epsilon, and there were times when fans would just walk right up to him and gush before asking to take a photo or get an autograph.

Simon spoke up. "Have a seat, Mr. Westley. I don't think any of us were aware that Oliver had such a following back at Yale."

"Thank you, Mr. Copeland, and please call me Nathan." He sat down, crossed his legs and waved for the waitress.

"You may call me Simon, and I'm certain Oliver won't mind you calling him by his first name. Right, Oliver?"

Oliver snapped out of his contemplation. "Yes, of course. It's nice to meet you, Nathan."

Nathan ordered a Tom Collins when the waitress returned, then settled back in his seat, smiling expectantly at the brothers, as if waiting for something.

"So, Nathan, what have you been doing with yourself since graduation? What are your plans?" Simon asked.

Oliver was glad to have his brother there. Simon was a great conversationalist. Being a Copeland, and the CEO of the family business, Oliver should have been used to being treated like a celebrity, but even so he was a bit overwhelmed by the eagerness of this young man.

"I've been making the rounds in Manhattan looking for a position. But what I actually plan to do is start my own company. I've found I have a great deal of talent in investing in others' ideas and helping them grow. I like technology, software, hardware, new apps, and that sort of thing. I've already made a tidy sum even while I was still earning my MBA."

Belle Cay wasn't exactly the technology center of the world, thought Oliver, and the tiny island was practically a bedroom community. "Isn't Belle Cay a little far from the hubbub of the city? I thought you might want to be closer to Wall Street."

"Well, I hadn't planned on living here, but I just fell in love with it. I bought a great place here and a penthouse in Manhattan. I can come home on the weekends." Emboldened by the questions, Nathan Westley spent the next twenty minutes talking about himself and sparing no compliments.

It seemed to Oliver that someone so eager to meet him might have wanted to know a little more about him. At the same time, though, he was thankful not to be subject to an interrogation under the hot light of the man's previous adulating attention. He listened politely, doing his best to commit all the details of Nathan's life story to memory; if something came up later, he did not want to appear ignorant and the exercise of trying to remember things was always good for his brain.

Nathan finally stood. "May I give you my card? I would really enjoy getting together to talk sometime. I have to go, though; I'm meeting with a decorator in half an hour." Nathan pulled a card from a slim silver case and handed it to Oliver, who in turn handed his card to Nathan.

"I look forward to it," Oliver told him.

"Well," said Simon winking at his brother after the man had walked away. "I guess women aren't the only ones swooning over you."

Oliver laughed, and though being the focus of such attention had made him uncomfortable, he also thought it was nice to be known as who he had once been instead of who he was now. He made a note in his phone to call Nathan Westley tomorrow.

4

The private gym in the Copeland Enterprises headquarters in Belle Cay was dark at 5:12 in the morning as Oliver arrived. The motion-controlled lights flickered on at his entrance. To ensure he would have no witnesses for his early tries at running, he locked the door behind him. He was on a new fitness plan in order to become the man he had been before. Sarah had gone shopping with him to buy some workout clothes and had teased him, saying he was handsome enough and maybe he was having a mid-life crisis. He wondered if he *was* having a mid-life crisis, and found that he honestly didn't care. This would be good for him, good for Sarah, good for the rest of his family, and good for

Copeland Enterprises.

Alec, the man hired to run the company's gym, had begged him not to work out alone, but had reluctantly given in when Oliver signed a waiver. Alec's attitude had to be commended, but was Oliver really going to sue his own company if he had an accident in the gym? He had to do this, and he had to do it alone. He couldn't and wouldn't let anyone think he needed help.

Looking at the indoor track made his stomach tie up in knots. "I can do this," he thought as he stretched. "Heck, I used to run the bleachers. I can run a silly track." After his stretches, he stepped onto the start/finish line, started the timer on his new fitness watch, and began his run. But it wasn't much of a run. It was a hitching, slow approximation of a run. He kept going anyway. Pride compelled him to continue even though his mind seemed to take delight in conjuring up one gruesome scene after another of what might happen to him while he was here alone.

Pain raced through his ankles and knees before quickly moving up through his hips to his chest. He was an athlete, and a little pain had never stopped him nor would it. The track loomed ahead and slanted from side to side, trying to upset his delicate balance. Breathing became difficult and his eyesight turned white as brightness replaced the track. Maybe his body was no longer strong, but his willpower was like Goliath. He refused to stop, until suddenly his body made the decision for him. He lost his balance and crashed to the ground, landing hard on his left leg.

Oliver opened his eyes and saw he had made it to his starting point. He stopped the timer and focused his eyes on the watch: Four minutes forty-seven seconds for a quarter of mile. "Okay, well, nowhere to go but up from here." He was speaking aloud through heavy breaths, and his voice echoed back to him in the large, empty fitness center.

Getting up took some time, but he tested his leg and had no trouble walking on it. He took a long draught from his water bottle, reset the timer to zero, and began again. The hitch was worse, and the pace was painfully slow, yet he did not relent. The hurting didn't decrease, but he did find his breathing eased a little. Another lap completed: slightly over five minutes for that one. Walking would have been faster. Those two laps were more than he had done in years. He wasn't sure whether to be proud of himself for the effort or disappointed at how poorly he had done. It was a strange and conflicting feeling.

Glad no one was around, and gladder still the security guards were downstairs or on rounds, Oliver hobbled to his office and private bathroom. He turned on the steam in the sauna. How long had it been since he had used it after a workout? Seven, eight years? He cringed at the idea of using the sauna in the gym. No matter how well cleaned, dirty people sat and sweated out their toxins into the wood. Just the thought made him squirm. The throbbing of his knee caused him to examine it closer; it was swollen and the deep red color promised to turn black and blue. He supposed he ought to have iced it. Where were the ice packs? He wasn't sure if he had one in his office refrigerator. Maybe after he was changed he would go back to the fitness center and check the attached clinic for one.

Stepping from the sauna into the shower made him wince with pain, but once under the hot flow of water, he imagined all the pain being washed away. He merely stood there for several minutes and relished in the clean hot cascade of water. Finally, he scrubbed himself until his skin fairly sparkled.

What a satisfying feeling to know he had run, or at least sort-of run, even only half a mile, and then to be fresh, dressed, and ready for the day. It was just after 8:00 in the morning and the cafeteria would be serving breakfast. Oliver made his way downstairs. He was hungry, hungry as a horse. Did they serve bearies downstairs? He could eat one. Working out had meant sacrificing breakfast with Sarah and his mother at Cumberland Manor. He would have to make it up to each of them. Perhaps he would take them out to eat tonight.

The cafeteria was upscale and offered a different menu of foods each day prepared by chefs. It was one of the small touches that kept productivity up and allowed all employees, from executives to mail room clerks, to enjoy a nice meal. Oliver glanced at the day's menu and chose the fresh strawberry protein smoothie. He would tell Asha he had eaten a straw bearie for breakfast. His knee was shooting sharp pains up toward his hip, making his limp more pronounced, but rather than sit, Oliver went back upstairs to drink his smoothie in the privacy and quiet of his office. He realized that he could have ordered up, or even had his assistant Marcus get something for him. He smiled and greeted the few employees he passed on the way to his office. It was good for them to see him around the building maybe it even stroked his ego a little to have employees respectfully greet him.

By the time Oliver reached his office, his knee was screaming in agony at him. He reached his desk and sat with a sigh of relief, rifling through his desk drawer for the ibuprofen and swallowing them with some smoothie. The laptop flashed with emails containing files, proposals, and ideas waiting for his approval or disapproval. His calendar blinked to remind him of scheduled meetings. He checked the calendar first, even though Marcus, when he arrived, would once again go over the day's agenda. Two meetings were on the day's to-do list, one in an hour and the other over lunch, and then prepping for Monday's board meeting. Okay, not too bad; he could handle that. He dialed Cumberland Manor and asked for his mother before remembering he should have dialed her cell phone. Regardless which number he dialed, though, he knew he would reach her.

Catherine's voice came over the line. "Oliver, is everything alright?"

"It's fine. I just thought I would take you and Sarah out to eat tonight."

"Honey, we've got Deborah and Ash and Simon and Denise coming tonight." Catherine paused and her tired voice sounded a little happier. "But I'll tell you what, I'm a little under the weather, so why don't I let everyone know we're eating at the club tonight and I can bow out and get some rest. Shall I have Nisha make reservations for you?"

"I'm sorry you're not well, Mother. Are you alright?"

"I'm fine, dear. I'm just tired. I'm very happy to get an early night." Her voice sounded more than merely tired to Oliver; she sounded fatigued and even fragile.

"Okay," he said, acquiescing to her request. "Yes, have Nisha make the reservations, and text them to Marcus and me. Also have her please let everyone else know. Thank you, Mother."

Marcus walked in to the office just as Oliver was hanging up. "Good morning, Mr. Copeland. How are you?" The trim man held his tablet out with his fancy stylus in midair, ready to work. His bright blue suit accentuated his deep ebony skin and black eyes.

"Fine, thanks," said Oliver, trying not to wince as he moved his leg.

"Are you in pain? What happened?" Marcus had caught his stifled wince. That attention to small details was part of what made Marcus excel at his job.

"Ah, I'm fine. I upped my workout and my muscles are sore. Nothing to be concerned about."

Yet Marcus was obviously concerned. "Are you sure? Let me get you an ice pack." He headed toward the first-aid kit stowed in a bookcase cabinet and started to activate an instant ice-pack.

Oh, yeah, that's where they were. "Marcus, please don't. I'm fine. It's nothing. Stop being a nurse and start being an assistant. What's on the agenda today?"

Marcus immediately obeyed; he knew better than to fuss over his employer. With the knee nonsense out of the way, the two men got on to the day's business.

5

Oliver trailed behind his family as they stepped onto *Freedom's Joy*. The cruiser was huge and weighted down at every corner with luxurious woods and ornate trim; for all of Gordon Sumner's talk of regattas, this was not a racing yacht. The captain, Martin Tripp, stood near the gangway and helped the women step onto the deck. He didn't look much older than twenty-five, but his skin was obviously the product of years on boat decks, bearing a deep tan that shone against the navy and white of his monogrammed uniform. He welcomed each of the Copelands with a Maine-accented deep voice and a wide smile. Oliver watched Sarah flirtatiously chatting with Martin as she waited for Oliver to reach the entryway. She had canceled her plans immediately for the chance to spend the day on the water. His daughter was vivacious, charming, and as beautiful as any fifteen-year-old could be. Oliver felt a bit protective over her as he switched his attention to the yacht's captain and interrupted the conversation. "Hello! Well, she is a beauty, isn't she? I am looking forward to a tour."

Martin Tripp's concentration quickly moved to Oliver. He smiled broadly. "Welcome aboard *Freedom's Joy*. I will be happy to take you on a tour. I'm Captain Tripp, and if you need anything please do not hesitate to find a crew member or me and we will be happy to help."

Oliver carefully stepped over the gap and gained his balance on the deck. "Very good, thank you. I see you met my daughter Sarah." Emphasizing the word daughter, Oliver hoped the man understood the implied warning.

"Daddy," said Sarah as she kissed his cheek, "may I go to the forecastle, please?"

Oliver checked with the captain, who nodded assent. "Yes, but please be careful."

"Thank you, Daddy!" She trotted to the aftmost deck of the cruiser to see if it would be a suitable place for looking out on the water later.

Oliver steered himself toward the others, who were already aboard. He tried to hide the pain of his now badly bruised knee. Every muscle in his body ached from his workout yesterday and each movement made him want to scream. He wanted to sit down but couldn't show his weakness to anyone. "Isn't the cruiser a little large for racing?" he asked Martin. "I thought you were hired for the regattas."

Gordon was approaching, and answered for the captain. "Well, I plan to have Captain Tripp race my daysailer, the *Regal Phyllis II*. *Freedom's Joy* is for cruises, gatherings, and winters living like a king in Panama. I'll be touring everyone in about an hour; I'm expecting a few more guests." Gordon left Oliver with a small group of people listening to Vera talk about getting tenure at the university.

Vera saw Oliver and interrupted herself, "Oh, Oliver, I am so happy to see you! I enjoyed dinner the other night very much. I do love spending time with you." She touched his shoulder as she spoke. Oliver couldn't tell whether she noticed his embarrassment at her attention and its implications, but she removed her hand. "Well, Cumberland Manor is always a joy to visit. Do you know that several of the pieces in the museum are actually on loan from the Copeland family? Still, the collection you have there is impressive. I think I may try to talk you into putting a few more pieces in the museum on a rotation."

Oliver looked around, hunting for a reason to excuse himself from Vera and the small group surrounding her. He had a terrible mental image of her pulling him in and sucking the life out of him, and there was no way he would ever let anyone hurt him the way Kelly had hurt him. She had crushed his heart, his body, and his pride. He didn't need a woman; he was fine without romance. Yet no escape route appeared to him.

He did notice when Lucy Treadway, a beautiful woman who also attended his church, joined the group. She smiled at Oliver and waved as Vera continued speaking about something or other. Oliver had stopped listening. Now he watched the graceful Lucy as she pushed her flowing obsidian hair behind her ear and lifted it off her neck for a moment. Her long neck sported a simple gold cross necklace, and Oliver found he couldn't take his eyes off it. He had lost complete track of what Vera or anyone else in the little group was saying. Simon arrived out of the blue, pulling Oliver from his thoughts.

"Oliver, I need to talk to you." He turned to the group. "I hope you don't mind me stealing my brother. I am sure we will get the chance to talk later." Oliver glanced over his shoulder to see a crestfallen look on Vera's face as Simon ushered him away. "I will do my utmost to keep you clear of her today," Simon assured him.

"Thank you," said Oliver with obvious relief, walking beside his brother along the boat's railings. "She has begun to grate on me. I don't enjoy feeling a dislike for another person, but I do."

Simon smiled. "I love that about you, Ollie. You've always looked for the good in people and always found it. You can find whatever there is to like in Vera, I'm sure. But I think Denise is going to set her up with Felix Demarco; her attentions will go to him, and then it will once again be safe for you to be friends with her." He stopped speaking for a moment then said, "Your limping pretty badly. Are you hurt?"

"I'm not sure I know Felix Demarco. I hope he enjoys listening more than talking" Oliver observed, hoping to turn the conversation in that direction so he didn't have to answer Simon's question. He could tell from Simon's skeptical raised eyebrow that there was no fooling his brother, though. "I've begun running again and I'm not quite used to it yet. My muscles are sore."

Simon wasn't satisfied with that answer. "And…?"

Oliver blushed with shame, turning to look out at the water. "And I tripped yesterday and bruised my knee. I'm fine."

"Why don't we let Denise look at it? It could be sprained."

Oliver felt anger rise like a grenade about to explode in his brain and burst out of his mouth. He squelched it, hard. The checked anger burned in his stomach but the little bit of freedom he felt around his family allowed some to escape his lips like steam from a kettle of boiling water. In a fierce whisper that threatened to grow louder with each word, he said, "I am fine. I'm not a child. In fact, I am quite grown, and older than you. It is a bruise, not a sprain. I don't need people taking care of me."

Simon almost managed to hide the hurt feelings from his face. "Oliver, I know that. I'm sorry. I was and am concerned for you. I will never not care about you and your welfare; I just thought that since we have a doctor in the family, you could let Denise make sure it's only a bruise and doesn't need treatment."

Oliver was already regretting what he'd said; he knew that Simon had not meant anything by the offer, and he hated being so defensive. More than that, he hated that he lacked the self-control to hold back his anger. "I'm sorry, Simon. I really am just fine. Let's get something to drink; I'll pop a couple of ibuprofen, and we can take a walk and check on Sarah."

"Sounds great," Simon agreed, and the two headed for the bartender.

A seltzer for Simon and lemonade for Oliver in their hands, the brothers headed toward the forecastle as the cruiser headed out toward the water. They met Sarah partway, and she came running up to hug her father and uncle. "Daddy, we need to go out more on the yacht. Wouldn't it be wonderful to throw a dinner party just for family for my Sweet Sixteen eve?"

"Your birthday is such a big event it has an eve now?" joked Simon, as he purposely mussed the teen's hair.

"Uncle Simon," she said, sounding as serious as possible, "a person only turns sixteen once. I am embarking on adulthood, and the party will be so big I won't get a chance to have the time with each of you that I long to have. I think it is a brilliant idea." She smoothed the hair her uncle had disheveled.

Stifling a laugh at the attempted seriousness of Sarah's monologue, Oliver chimed in. "I think a family party sounds fine, but a dinner cruise with all the little ones isn't a good idea. You can join your uncle the next time he goes out, maybe even train to help the crew in the races. We will plan for a special evening at Cumberland for the family."

"Fine, Daddy, but not at Cumberland. I mean, I eat dinner there nearly every night. This has to be special. Let's jet somewhere spectacular!"

A slight smile caught the corner of Oliver's mouth. "Fine, Princess. We will find something wonderful, but probably not far enough away that it requires a jet."

Satisfied, Sarah left to join Lindsey and Ashley Wellington and Maya Treadway. Lindsey and Maya were both in Sarah's class, while Ashley was a year ahead of them. Oliver supposed their talk would be all about the upcoming party.

"You spoil that girl, you know," said Simon.

"I don't think she's spoilable." Oliver retorted, trying not to be on the defensive. "Besides, I have many rules and she follows them all faultlessly. She doesn't have her mother around; I have to make that up to her. She is a good girl and a great help to me. I'm aware of her manipulations; I simply choose to ignore some of them. That's all."

"She is a good girl; you're right. Anyway, it's not my place to give you a hard time about this. I think Cathy could ask for the Empire State Building and I'd figure out how to get it for her." Simon paused, took a breath. "But you getting Kelly out of her life was beneficial. Kelly was hurting you, and even if she never lifted a finger against Sarah, the situation was bad for her. Kelly's leaving was a good thing."

"I don't know if losing your mother is ever entirely good. Sarah has Mother, Denise, and Deborah, but it's not the same." Oliver put his empty glass on the tray of a passing waiter. "Kelly is broken. She never learned to love herself, so how could she be expected to love anyone else? Even so, Sarah was the only thing that made Kelly be even a little bit unselfish. It might be good for both of them if Kelly would come back into her daughter's life."

"Big brother, you are a spectacular person. Of all the people in the world, you have a right to hate Kelly the most, and I think you hate her least of all."

Oliver touched Simon's shoulder, stopping their walk. "I loved her once; I don't think I could hate her now. She gave me Sarah."

The two headed toward their own mother, who was relaxing on a deck chair and watching the blue of the water grow deeper as the yacht headed out towards the sea. Oliver looked at her, and love for her filled him. She looked regal even merely sitting in the sun in her white culottes, a white silk blouse, and dark sunglasses. Her thick gray hair was swept up under her large brimmed hat. The brothers kissed each kissed a cheek simultaneously and she hugged them happily in return.

6

Pain in Oliver's stomach threatened to tear his insides apart as apprehension gripped him. Pride thrust the fear aside and ordered him to the starting line of the track. He pressed the start button on the mp3 player at his waist, then the start button on the fitness watch, and at last he began his morning run. A deep voice with a British accent recited the Psalms to a background of Chopin, and the pleasant sound filled his ears and calmed his mind. He had run every morning except Sunday for the past week. The run was working its way into his routine. About halfway through the first lap, the hurt came. As he neared the start of the second lap, the pain hit him hard as his lungs felt as if they would burst, his side exploded into agony, and his sight went white. He refused to stop running. Pain was nothing. He had never allowed a little discomfort to stop him, and he never would.

Several minutes passed before his side stopped screaming and began whimpering. His aching subsided as he broke through "the wall" and gained his second wind. Chopin's *Étude No 7 in C major, Toccata* sang in his ear and the British voice spoke of God's steadfast love overcoming David's transgressions. But Oliver's mind repeated a mantra of "I can do this. I can do all things through Him who strengthens me. I can do this." He knew that the verse he quoted had nothing to do with running bleachers or climbing mountains. It was about living in any circumstance, about enduring suffering or living with all needs met and still depending on God. But for him, living with the circumstances of his injuries meant overcoming them and being his old self.

Only twenty feet ahead of him, the finish line waited and taunted him with its own refrain, "No you can't." But today would be the day he finished his run without walking. Today would be the day he tried a third lap. "I can do this." He wanted to say it out loud but he had no spare breath. The calm and steady voice pleaded with God to prove him and try him. "For your steadfast love is before my eyes," it said. Oliver closed his eyes and imagined God before him as a bright purple light. He stopped his mantra and prayed, "Lord help me do this, please." He opened his eyes again and there was his finish line. He ran past it and felt as if he had won an Olympic race. That triumphant feeling lasted only a minute as he stopped the timer and read 7:33. The time was an improvement and should have made him happy, but he was busy comparing himself to his old days when 3:33 might have been okay.

Oliver drank his water, gathered his things, and left the gym. He told himself he had done a good job, and the next day he would try for two and half laps. He walked to his office and turned off the mp3 player to enjoy the quiet of the building. The stillness calmed his spirit as much as Chopin could lift it. Deliberately slowing his breaths, he counted to six and breathed in, then to eight as he exhaled until he reached his office feeling peaceful.

After he was showered and dressed, Oliver sat down at his desk, ordered a greens juice with protein, and checked the day's agenda. He paused from checking his emails as the building came alive around him. The hallway lights came on, men and women filtered in, and the sound created a pleasant buzz. Soon, he knew, the buzz would be too loud for him, and he would close the office door to insulate himself from the chaos it created in his brain. The woman from the cafeteria approached his open door and knocked. He smiled, looked down at the post-it note by his keyboard, read 'café delivery girl brown hair- Shelly,' and said, "Good morning, Shelly; come in. How are you today?"

"Fine, thanks," she said as she entered and gave him his juice. "I finally got little Mike into that school, and now I only have to worry about getting him the right uniforms. How are you, Mr. Copeland?"

"That's great," Oliver said, glad to have someone give an honest answer rather than the usual fine-thanks. While she might have appreciated a real answer from him, it never occurred to him to share personal and possibly embarrassing details with anyone outside of his family. "I'm really well today, thank you."

Shelley left, and he was alone in his ordered and quiet office with the hum of the business as a pleasant backdrop. He read his emails, marking those which required action as unread. That ended up being the majority of them. He came to one from Nathan Westley and realized he had never called the young man as he had planned. The email thanked Oliver for meeting with him and requested an appointment to meet once more to discuss a business proposition. Oliver wrote a reply offering a lunch meeting, leaving the date and time blank, and saved the email without sending so that Marcus could fit it into his schedule.

Marcus arrived just then, looking debonair as ever in a stylish gray pinstriped suit. While Oliver was still thinking of it, he had Marcus fill in the details for the lunch meeting and send the email. He was interested in getting to know Nathan better, and he was also curious about whatever business proposition he might have.

"You have a meeting with Langley Barnett this morning at 9:15." Marcus said somewhat hesitantly.

Oliver sighed. Langley had worked for Copeland Enterprises for twenty-six years and had been acting CEO when Oliver had had been out of commission. Unfortunately, for some unknown reason, the man thought very little of Oliver. Meetings with him were always difficult as Langley's attitude toward Oliver seemed inflexible. He had not been happy that Oliver had "inherited" the position from his father rather than earning it.

Yet, Oliver reminded himself, he had earned it. He had worked alongside his father even when he had been a high school student. He had begun as a junior executive and had earned his promotions. Certainly he had been groomed to be the CEO, and that fact had never been hidden from anyone, but he had not just walked off the street to take the title.

At the same time, though, Oliver reminded himself of Langley's loyalty to the company, and to Oliver's father personally. He reminded himself how hard Langley had worked and all the good he had done for the company in Oliver's three-and-a-half-year absence from work. He looked over at Marcus, who was watching him expectantly. "Please ensure we are served the coffee he likes, and make sure Lisa knows we are not to be interrupted except for emergencies. You will, of course, stay here and take notes."

"Yes sir." Marcus checked the time and called Lisa to arrange for the coffee. Lisa Daniels was Marcus' secretary – no, Oliver amended, not secretary anymore, administrative assistant. By default that made her Oliver's administrative assistant as well.

She was a short and stout woman who worked hard and seemed only able to speak about business in a business-like manner. She was quiet and headstrong. Perhaps those qualities were what enabled her to perform so well at a job which could easily have been split between two people. She wouldn't have another administrative assistant because she was a perfectionist who trusted no one but herself to do her job properly.

"Perhaps Lisa should take notes during the meeting," Marcus suggested. "You know he'll make some comment about me doing your job for you, or something else tactless."

"I prefer you be here, Marcus. Besides, maybe today is the day when Langley Barnett chooses not to belittle anyone or realizes that I never was, nor ever will be, a threat to him. He has the second highest position in a world-wide company, and that is as high as he can go."

Marcus left the office and Oliver read an update from Eito Kita, the top man in the Tokyo office. His mind was not entirely on the e-mail. Reading the same paragraph for the third time, Oliver gave up on it for the time being. Despite his words to Marcus, he was apprehensive about the meeting with Langley. The older man always made him nervous. Even as a teenager, Oliver had been intimidated by Langley's size and militaristic demeanor. His service in the Marines was something Barnett was and should have been proud of, but he used it to further debase Oliver every chance he got.

Marcus knocked on the open office door and entered followed by Langley Barnett. The man was exceptionally large. He was tall, about 6'7" was Oliver's guess, and had the musculature of a body builder. His salt-and-pepper hair was worn in the traditional Marine high-and-tight style. He took the offered seat, which disappeared beneath his bulk. Lisa walked in with coffee and poured three cups without speaking. She knew how each man took his coffee and didn't ask who wanted it. Langley drank his black, shaking his head as Lisa added milk and sugar to Oliver's cup.

Oliver needed to speak, but his tense brain refused to provide the words. He smiled, pretended to take a sip from his cup, and breathed in for a count of six, then put his cup down and exhaled for a count of eight. His brain switched on and he willed it to stay on. "Langley, what can I do for you today?"

Barnett wasted no time on pleasantries.

"You need to put more money into the technology division. CE is living in the past. Not only should we be acquisitioning new technologies, we should be looking into more R&D. Don't tell me we can't do it. I've looked into it. As CFO, I know we can. We have three outlets for stationery supplies, and at least one if not two of those can be reorganized and the money funneled to technology." He spoke as if chastising a naughty child.

Oliver chose not to hear the reprimanding tone, and ignored the man's deliberate use of acronyms, which Oliver felt sure was meant to confuse him. He continued his rhythmic breathing and finally said. "I think you're right about expanding our technological markets. I've been working on it, actually. I've got a few people in mind to come onboard and several new pitches to…" he lost the word for a moment. Panic tried to seize him. What was the word? It wouldn't come. He had to find some other way to voice his thought and even that didn't want to emerge. Inhale for six, exhale for eight.

He finally said, "think over." It had only been a momentary pause and most people would have missed it, but he thought Langley might have caught it. Turning to Marcus, he said, "Mr. Temple, please e-mail the Kensington, Thompson, and Vasquez files to Mr. Barnett this afternoon after I've finished with them." Turning back to Barnett, he added, "In fact, I have a lunch appointment today with a man I'm considering bringing in, who has some great new ideas about this stuff." He didn't know a single one of Nathan's ideas, but he felt that at this point keeping his momentum was the important thing. "I'm glad we're on the same page. Now, if there is nothing else, we both have plenty of work to get done." Oliver stood, making it clear the unnecessary meeting was over.

Langley Barnett stood. "Yes, good. We're both on the same page. Maybe if you would communicate more, or allow the division more autonomy, I wouldn't have to waste my time checking on you."

"It is not in your job description to check on me." Oliver's annoyance was barely contained. "This is my company; I check on you." He stopped speaking and sat down, feeling that anything further would have come out in shouting.

Marcus opened the door and showed Langley out. Closing the door behind him, he said, "Every time that man is in here, he either complains that you're too hands-off or that you're too hands-on. If you'll pardon me saying so, sir, he pushes my buttons."

"He pushes mine, too." Oliver continued counting his breaths to relax. "Let's get to work."

7

Oliver watched Nathan Westley approach the table of the Yacht Club's restaurant. The younger man wore an expensive suit, and his high-priced Omega watch was prominently displayed on his wrist. Nathan smiled a greeting, his teeth almost as shiny as the black leather on the suitcase he carried. "Thank you for meeting me, Mr. Copeland."

"Call me Oliver, please." Oliver offered him the seat opposite his.

"Thank you, Oliver. I'm excited to tell you my ideas. I believe I could make you a rather large sum of money." Nathan wasted no time before getting down to business, which was exactly how Oliver wanted it. Oliver had never been fond of small talk, and he appreciated skipping the superfluous chatter.

Pulling a file folder from his briefcase, Nathan was about to begin his presentation when the server, an unobtrusive college-aged young man, took their lunch orders. Nathan then spoke enthusiastically for several minutes about his latest idea, a cross-device app which would act as an assistant, organizing contacts, schedules, and receipts. "This app not only will take and file the information from a business card with a simple snap of the camera, it will search social media and find profiles matching the contact information. It will do the same with manually entered information. I'm working on matching the information to news stories and public records from multiple sources as well." He continued his pitch for at least another fifteen minutes.

Oliver listened and nodded but didn't interrupt. Much of what the man said involved terms Oliver didn't know; technology was something he enjoyed as a consumer but the jargon that went with its development was not in his vocabulary. He was not on any social media sites, despite Sarah's efforts to drag him into the twenty-first century's obsession with online posting, sharing, liking, and poking, whatever that was.

Nathan handed Oliver a small packet of papers with the information he had shared. "This is going to revolutionize business networking and give users a glimpse into the side of their contacts they are not immediately sharing. I estimate that the market for this app will go beyond the men and women of the business world. I see college and high school students using it both to stay on top of their studies and to enjoy social media in a new depth. Oliver, this is a huge opportunity. I only need some capital to fund the final development and production."

"Nathan, I like the idea. I need to look into it, and also into the patents. Do you have a prototype yet? I wouldn't mind testing it." Oliver flipped through the packet, Nathan had given him. "I plan to let my lawyers and the researchers at Copeland's tech division look through this before I give you a final answer, if that's alright."

"I don't have a prototype ready just yet. Yes, have your lawyers look it over. I have obtained some of the patents already; the paperwork is in there." Nathan took a bite of coq-au-vin, which had arrived some minutes prior and had probably cooled considerably as he'd spoken. "On a personal note, I have tickets to the philharmonic next weekend. They will be performing Beethoven's Ninth. I would be really pleased if you might consider joining me."

Oliver smiled. "Beethoven's *Symphony Number Nine* is my favorite piece of music. Thank you, but I have box seats. Why don't you join me instead? We can talk more then."

"I would love to! Thanks. I guess it's true: great minds think alike!" Nathan took a sip of wine. "I tell you what, how about I buy dinner beforehand?"

"Okay, it sounds like a plan. Send the information with the reservations to my assistant at this number." Oliver handed him a card with Marcus' information. "He will let you know what time my car will pick you up."

8

Dinner had been wonderful. Oliver ate the delectable roast squab and black truffles with a delight he did not often have for food. But Le Saveur was a favorite restaurant, and squab a favorite food, and truffles enhanced just about any recipe. "Mother would love this dish; I might have one sent home to her. I'm sorry you couldn't meet her tonight. She normally comes with me. The symphony is one of the things we have done together since I was about eight years old, I think."

"I'm sorry I couldn't meet her. I've read so much about your mother. It is no wonder you are the man you are. She is quite amazing according to the papers." Nathan flicked a truffle off his own squab, making Oliver wonder why he had ordered something that came with the expensive fungus.

"She is as good as the good the papers report, and much more. You'll meet her soon." Oliver finished his food and rested his knife across his plate as the waiter appeared and placed the bill next to him.

Nathan reached across the table and took the small leather folder. He opened it and then reached into his inside jacket pocket. A look of shame crossed his face and he checked various other pockets. "I am so sorry. I-I seem to have forgotten my wallet. Let me make a call and see if I can get someone to bring it here. Please forgive me."

"It's not a problem; you can get it next time." Oliver took the folder back and placed his card in it with just a glance at the total. "I don't want to miss any of the music."

Nathan practically poured out apologies before Oliver stopped him. "It's fine, really. I'm glad to get to know you a little more, and I don't mind. Everyone makes mistakes."

The theater was alive with the whir of voices and sound of the orchestra warming up. It was an agreeable sound, but it was also a sound of barely controlled chaos. Oliver concentrated on the pleasantness of it as he followed the usher to his box. On the way to their seats, the harmony was broken by the discordant sound of Vera Sumner's voice. "Oliver! Oh! I was hoping to see you this evening!"

Oliver tried not to visibly recoil from the unexpected hug that went along with her greeting. He forced a smile. "It's a pleasure to see you Vera."

Next to Vera, a short man with Mediterranean features wrapped his arm around hers. Oliver recognized him but couldn't place him. The man was about to speak before Vera spoke for him. "Oliver this is my friend Felix Demarco. Felix, this is my dear family friend, Oliver Copeland." The two men shook hands but neither was able to say a word. "The Copelands have been friends for as long as I can remember," Vera continued. "We practically grew up together. I still remember Oliver running around in short pants. Well, it looks as if we need to get to our seats. It was so good seeing you. Wish your mother well for me, please. Come along, Felix, dear."

Oliver watched them leave and hoped the two would hit it off. She had never even given him a chance to introduce Nathan. "Well, I'm sorry I couldn't introduce you to Vera

Sumner. Her aunt and uncle are family friends."

"No apologies necessary," replied Nathan as they reached the private box.

The men took their seats just as the orchestra quieted and the din of voices grew louder with anticipation. The lights dimmed and a hush spread like a cresting wave over the crowd. At last the curtain opened. The conductor was introduced, and he stepped onto the stage, walking like a peacock to his place in front of the large orchestra. He raised his arms and held them high for a few moments. Oliver leaned forward in anticipation. Then, with the conductor's movement, the music began.

The music was like light shining through the bars of a dark and damp dungeon. It warmed the cell and showed the prisoner inside hope. It spoke of a forgotten life outside, a life that might not be so far beyond his reach. The second movement brought attention to the thick door of the prison chamber. The melody rattled the handle and shook the locked exit with the desire for freedom. With the third movement, the captive recognized the key he held in his hand. It turned in the lock. But it was the final movement, the *Ode to Joy*, which swung the door open. Fresh air and sunlight filled the space as Oliver flew out of his confinement. The song was wings for his soul, and took him higher and higher until he could see the entirety of the world was his. He soared ever upward and knew the universe waited for him to take it.

Tears flowed unchecked down Oliver's cheeks in the dark theater. As the conductor stepped off the rostrum, Oliver wiped his face quickly with his handkerchief and stood to his feet in applause. Nathan joined him, as did most of the crowd. The conductor bowed repeatedly as if it were his own composition, then presented the soloists and the choir while the audience continued its ovation.

After the curtains closed and the crowd began to disperse, Nathan began speaking. "That was wonderful! It was such a thrill, really, to have such a vantage point to the stage."

Oliver wished the man would stop talking for a few minutes so he could remain in fellowship with the music for a little longer. His soul wanted to stay in flight and not be dragged down to earth just yet. But Nathan continued his accolades for the orchestra, conductor, and Oliver. "Yes, it was very nice," Oliver finally agreed. He understood the high that music could give a person; he experienced and expressed his differently than Nathan and didn't want to take it away from the younger man.

After the crowd had thinned, the two men left the box and went to the waiting car. All the while, Nathan's exuberance for the performance continued. In the car as they were about to arrive to his hotel, he finally calmed down from the euphoria. "Shall we grab a drink?"

"No, not tonight. I prefer to go directly home, but let's get lunch again soon." The car arrived at the Belle Cay Hotel. "Call Marcus and he'll set it up."

"Yes, good, and don't forget it will be my treat next time." Nathan got out of the limo with a wave and a smile.

9

The doctor's office was decorated with rich mahogany wood and leather furniture in deep brown and tan colors. It should have conveyed warmth, but Dr. Kaplan's report made the space feel stark and cold. Catherine sat stunned in the chair across from the doctor. She had only felt this way a few times in her life. The last time had been when Simon had crashed his car and been grievously injured. Fear for her son's life had filled her with terror. It had happened before, too, when she had received the call about Oliver's skiing accident. The worst time had been when she had sat with her husband Arthur in an office much like this one and heard the news that he had leukemia. It had been so advanced that the doctor offered no hope, and he had lived a mere 43 days afterward.

Now she sat alone, listening to Dr. Kaplan as she explained heart disease. Catherine refused to cry. Growing up as Catherine Cumberland and living most of her life as Catherine Copeland had taught her to be exhibit nothing but stately quiet on the outside, regardless of the turmoil on the inside. But numbness emptied her of everything except the dignity she demonstrated.

"You have coronary microvascular disease and your heart has suffered a great deal of ischemia. It isn't pumping properly any longer, so your body isn't getting the oxygen-rich blood it needs. I will put you on some medication to keep your blood pressure down and allow the heart to not work so hard. You're also anemic, and I'll be treating that as well. I'm giving you nitroglycerin for chest pain and, if you like, something else for general pain. But I need you to get rest and avoid stress." Dr. Kaplan's practiced compassionate tone could not make up for her rehearsed speech, and it certainly could not infuse hope into her patient.

Catherine looked into the doctor's eyes,

"Will any of this help?"

"At this point, your comfort is the most important factor. I can place you on the transplant list, but I'm sorry to say that I'm uncertain whether you have that much time. I think the wiser option might be hospice. I can recommend several. I suggest you get a second opinion and talk with your family about your choices. A transplant and hospice care are not exclusive of one another, either. In fact, I would suggest you do both."

Catherine's demeanor hardened to keep her back straight and head high while her insides crumpled under the weight of the despair which had replaced the numbness. She stood. "Thank you, Dr. Kaplan. I will talk it over with my family. Place me on the transplant list. I do not intend to die just yet."

"You'll need to make another appointment for some more tests and education about how a transplant will work. Thank you, Mrs. Copeland. I'll see you at your next appointment." The doctor scribbled several prescriptions and placed them in Catherine's shaking hand. "Thank you," Catherine repeated as she left the office and walked blankly past the receptionist who waited to schedule her next appointment.

10

After church and the brief conversations with friends had ended, the Copelands and Levines were eager to get to the waiting cars that would carry them home to their weekly family day. Catherine was not feeling well, yet again. "Simon," she said, "please join me in my car, I'd like to have a conversation with you." She turned to Sarah, "Darling, please ride with Deborah or Denise."

Sarah stomped her foot but obeyed her grandmother without a word. She chose to ride with Deborah who would be driving her own car over sitting in the back of a limo with Denise and four children.

Simon kissed Denise and stepped into the back of his mother's car to join her. "What is it, Mother?" She looked so thin and drawn. "Are you opting out of family day again? We're gathering at my place today."

"I am," she said. Being at church made her feel as if she had just run a marathon. "But, I wanted to talk to you about Oliver. I'm worried about what will happen to him when I'm gone."

"Whoa! Mother, you have a long life still to live, you're not so old that you should be talking about your death as if it's any day now. Besides, Oliver is an adult. He doesn't need taking care of."

"He is, and he is responsible, caring, and smart. But, he is also compassionate, kind, and trusting. With his memory, with his benevolence… You know my eldest son chooses to think that every person has the same good intentions he does. I worry that someone may take advantage of him. He needs someone to look out for him, to be the bad cop to his good cop. I need you to just watch over him."

"I always watch out for him, Mother. I know what a sympathetic heart he has. But you forget how strong he is and how smart he is. He's okay."

"I know he's strong. He came back from that woman's abuse even stronger than he was before." Catherine refused to say the name of Oliver's ex-wife, even the thought of that woman gave her a sick taste in her mouth. "But, his distrust of love doesn't extend to a distrust of people in general. He is too trusting and I fear someone will see how this wealthy sweet man is vulnerable to their treachery."

Simon took Catherine's hand in his, raised it to his mouth and kissed it. "Mother, I love Oliver nearly as much as I love you, I will not let that happen to him. He doesn't like the idea of me as his protector, but I am. I do, and I will continue to watch over him. We watch over one another."

Oliver was still trying to figure out precisely how Nathan had convinced him to miss church and family time on Sunday morning, but here they both were at the club. Even stranger was the fact that he was wearing a bathing suit and sitting next to the sparkling pool, drinking some fruity tropical drink. Oliver rarely wore only a bathing suit in public, where others could judge his too-thin frame crisscrossed with a myriad of scars. His pale white skin spoke to his modesty and his dislike for an activity as dull as laying in the sun. But, he had to admit, he was enjoying himself.

Nathan was telling him some story about terrorizing his nanny as a child. Oliver had to laugh. Did every little boy feel the need to make his nanny's life as difficult as possible? Simon had gone out of his way to misbehave as a child, a teen, and even a young adult. Oliver had always felt that because his brother was so rebellious, he had to be the good son. He thought hard of a story to tell Nathan about his own childhood hijinks, yet nothing came to mind. At last he managed to say, "I hope your nanny got combat pay."

"She did. She retired on my twelfth birthday and went to live in the Caribbean or somewhere." Nathan laughed, "Poor Selma, she deserved to have a long and happy retirement after putting up with me."

The conversation lulled, and Oliver relished the temporary quiet. He inhaled for a count of six and exhaled for a count of eight as he enjoyed the moment and soaked up the sun. His phone rang, interrupting his bliss. He immediately felt guilt over his annoyance as he saw the caller was Sarah.

"Daddy, do I have to go to Copeland Gardens for lunch? Uncle Simon and Aunt Denise won't miss me. Grandmother isn't going. You aren't going. Uncle Ash is out of town. Please don't make me go. I'd rather go meet the girls for a movie."

"Sarah, dear, I will be there for dinner, and I expect to see you there as well. You will go to Uncle Simon's place and enjoy family day. Aunt Deborah was telling me she wanted to spend some time with you."

"You're missing family day. Grandmother is missing the third family day in a row!" As he listened to his daughter's protests, Oliver smiled slightly. He could imagine her stamping her foot. "It isn't fair!"

"I'm sorry, Princess; I had to have this business meeting today. I will be there for dinner. You are going, and I don't plan to miss another Sunday with you."

"Fine. Treat me like a child. Make me do what you won't do yourself." The phone clicked as Sarah ended the call without saying goodbye.

Guilt sapped all the pleasure out of the day. Oliver put his shirt on.

Nathan woke from his dozing, "Where are you going? I wanted to see if you had considered investing."

"I have some responsibilities at home. There are some things we need to discuss before I invest, but they will have to wait for another day." Oliver finished buttoning his shirt and picked up his phone to call Cuthbert, his driver and have him bring the car.

"Can't we talk first? I'm sure it won't be long."

Oliver sat back down on the edge of the lounge chair with a sigh. "I want to offer you a position at Copeland Enterprises. You'll have the financial backing to finish your app, as well as the freedom to develop other ideas. The salary and benefits are generous. And you could work out of Belleshore, or any of the offices around the world. A twenty-minute commute to Belleshore instead of hours back and forth to Manhattan is an advantage. Think it over. I need to go." Oliver stood up and put his pants on.

"Oliver, I appreciate it, but I don't want a position with a company. I want to make my own fortune. I want to enlarge your bank account, not some corporation's bottom line."

"We'll talk later." Oliver dialed the car and walked away. He headed toward the front of the club to meet Cuthbert.

"Excuse me, Mr. Copeland." Albert Knox, the country club manager, approached Oliver. "Will your friend be staying behind with your permission? He isn't a member."

Oliver hadn't realized Nathan was not a

club member. "Yes, he has my permission to enjoy one of my guest passes today."

"Is there a spending limit, sir?"

Only members could purchase anything from the club, as they were billed monthly rather than at the time of service. Had Nathan known that? Did he think he was somehow going to pay for the drinks and lunch they were to have enjoyed? "No limit, Albert. Let him enjoy the day, and make a recommendation for his membership with me as his sponsor."

"Yes, sir. Have a pleasant day sir."

Cuthbert was waiting for him with an open door. Oliver got into the car and headed toward Cumberland Manor to change before going to Copeland Gardens.

Simon's large home was aptly named Copeland Gardens. Its bucolic setting was filled with a tasteful variety of carefully landscaped flowers, trees, and plants. The home itself sat at the end of a long drive and was, respectfully, designed to be just a little less impressive than Cumberland Manor. The butler, whose name Oliver couldn't recall, led Oliver to the poolside patio where the family was finishing lunch.

Jackson saw his uncle and ran full force

into him, nearly knocking him down with his hug. None of the other children would be outdone, and Kyle, Misha, Cathy, and Asha soon joined in a group hug that resembled a football tackle as Oliver went down and the children piled on top of him. Their chatter melded together, but Oliver heard the main message: "Tell Mommy and Daddy we want to swim!" He kissed each child on the cheek and moved them one by one off his chest.

Sarah sat next to Deborah, playing with Daniel. "Daddy, you came!"

"I'm sorry. I shouldn't have missed church for a meeting and I certainly shouldn't have missed any of family day."

Simon helped his brother up and shooed the children away to play. "Come and sit down. Have you eaten?"

He wasn't hungry, but the drinks he'd had by the pool and his desire to gain muscle made him ask for a plate of food. "No, not yet. Thank you. Denise, Deborah, how are you?"

As conversation continued, Oliver's mind kept returning to Nathan Westley. He considered asking Simon's advice, but chose not to. Although Oliver had no need to grow wealthier, helping the young entrepreneur get started on his own life seemed like a good thing. He thought maybe he would do it.

He liked Nathan's attitude and energy. Nathan viewed him with a respect he normally only got from employees, and Oliver thought a genuine friendship had begun to develop as well. Nathan had faced several setbacks since arriving in Belle Cay, and had handled them gracefully. His wallet had been lost or stolen and his access to his accounts was temporarily frozen. He was not able to move into his new home as an inspection showed it required some work. Oliver had felt led to help the grateful man, although Nathan had fervently denied he needed any help. Oliver had even fronted him some money until things settled down.

The conversation turned toward Catherine. It seemed everyone was worried about her. "She won't talk about it, but I think she might be ill," Denise said. "She says she's fine. I'm not so sure."

Misha came running toward the group, "Jack won't let me play! He called me a baby!"

Simon stood. That was the cue for naptime. "Kids, come on in. It's time for a rest." Cathy and Asha quickly appeared, dolls in hand. "Jackson and Kyle! I want you here by the time I count to three or you will face consequences." He paused. "One…Two…

Thr…"

The two red-haired and freckled twins appeared with impish smiles. "Here we are!" They said simultaneously.

Denise got up but Simon said, "I've got this. Kids, say goodnight." He took all the children inside to put them down for naps.

11

A summer storm raged outside. The wind howled and sent the rain sideways so that it beat angrily against the window of Cumberland's library. Warm and dry inside, Catherine watched her family enjoy being who they were. Misha was sitting on his father's lap, raptly listening to the conversation taking place among the adults. Cathy and Asha were on the floor playing with Daniel as if he were their personal doll, and the baby seemed not to mind their attention. Jackson and Kyle played a board game in the corner. Sarah was drawing, either the design for a new dress or some plans for her party. The scene lifted Catherine's spirit with love, and also tore her soul apart with sadness that she might soon not be there.

She knew she needed to tell her family, or at least her sons, about the diagnosis and the prognosis, yet she couldn't abide bringing them this grief. She loved watching their joy. When Arthur was sick, each day had been fraught with sorrow and each moment had been overshadowed by his impending death. But knowing Arthur was ill had given them all a chance to say goodbye, and when he passed they had been ready for it, or as ready as one can be to lose a loved one. Did she owe them the chance to say goodbye? She just didn't know.

Of course, the adults and Sarah had all noticed she was sick. She had at last given in and told them that she was anemic and that she was being treated. That answer, a lie by omission, had placated her worried children. Denise had gone into overdrive, and much to Henri's chagrin had changed the chef's planned menus, filling them with healthy iron and protein-rich foods. Oliver had made sure she would be served breakfast in bed daily. Simon had taken over all gala, charity, and hosting duties for the remainder of the summer. What would they do when or if she told them the rest, the micro-whatever heart disease, the extensive heart damage, and the choice between a transplant and hospice?

She had looked into both options but had not yet done either. It all would be too real when she did. Did her sons deserve a say? Should they help her decide? Would it be easier to lean on them? She couldn't imagine leaning on anyone. She had relied on her father as a girl and her husband as a woman. As a widow, she had relied on no one. Quite the contrary, people depended on her. If there was need, Catherine met it. If someone was weak, Catherine was strong. How could she ask anyone to be strong for her, to meet her needs, to let her lean on them? No, she was Catherine Cumberland Copeland, and Catherine Cumberland Copeland was everyone else's pillar.

Every day, though, she grew a little weaker. Each day the pain was harder to conceal and more difficult to endure. She supposed she would have to make arrangements for hospice and a transplant soon. Surely, though, she would live; it couldn't be true that she was as sick as the doctor said. Her healthy new diet, some rest, and taking care of her blood pressure would do the trick, and before long she would be back in her place at The Arthur Copeland Foundation, the unofficial monarch of Belle

Cay, and the head of the Copeland family.

"Grandmother, look at this!" Sarah showed her the design of a sleek dress, floor length in the back and well above the knee in the front. "What color fabric should I use for it? Azure or plum?"

"Sarah, darling, it's lovely! I think you should go with the plum. You look so nice in purples. Or perhaps something lighter like a lilac would be wonderful on you."

"Okay, I think I have just the right fabric upstairs." Sarah went to her father. "Daddy, may I go upstairs and work on my new dress, please?"

Oliver, of course, consented, and the happy young lady went up to her sewing room as if she were headed to a corner of heaven.

Yes, Catherine decided she would have to overcome this illness, because she needed to see Sarah become a fashion designer and she needed to see the rest of her grandchildren grow into their future selves as well. It was too soon to leave, or even think of leaving them. God wouldn't take her away from all this just yet.

12

Glitter rained down from above, bubbles flowed from machines in every corner of the room, and lights danced in flashes of color. The crowd of elegantly dressed teenagers cheered as Oliver led Sarah onto the stage of the hotel ballroom. He winced at the great noise and visual pandemonium. Sarah soaked it in, naturally, since it was all for her. Watching his daughter smile as if her plans were a complete surprise and wave as if she were the queen of a nation, Oliver beamed with pride for her even as he wondered how anyone could thrive in the madness of the clamor and commotion. He inhaled for a count of six and exhaled for a count of eight.

Sarah squeezed his hand, "Daddy,

introduce me," she whispered into his ear and kissed his cheek.

Inhale. 1-2-3-4-5-6. Exhale. 1-2-3-4-5-6-7-8. He took the microphone from the emcee. "Ladies and gentlemen, thank you for joining us tonight as we celebrate my daughter Sarah Copeland's sixteenth birthday, and a milestone as she blossoms into womanhood." He looked at Sarah, "You will always be my baby girl. I think I might forever see you with golden hair tied up in colorful ribbons. But you are grown up, Princess. I am proud of the young woman you have become, and I look forward to seeing what you will do in this great wide world. Tonight, I'd like to present you with this gift, a token of a love I cannot fully express in words and always strive to express in actions." He traded the microphone for a slim flat box, which he opened to reveal a pearl necklace and matching earrings. The emcee held the mic near his face as he placed the necklace on his daughter. "A pearl necklace. A lovely exquisite and rare gift for a lovely, exquisite, and rare young woman."

"Thank you, Daddy!" Sarah hugged her father and took the mic from the emcee. "Now, let's dance!"

The crowd erupted and Oliver tried not to

flinch. The loudspeakers played a song he didn't know, and a spotlight stayed on him as he escorted Sarah to the dance floor for the Father-Daughter dance.

"Relax, Daddy. Just dance with me." Sarah reached up and put her arms around his neck.

With his hands on her waist, he willed the crowd away and looked at his daughter. Where had the time gone? How was she already sixteen? They swayed together. "I love you, Princess."

"I love you too Daddy."

The song changed to an upbeat tune and the dance floor was suddenly inundated with teenagers jumping, dancing, and cheering, many of them trying to get to Sarah to congratulate her and take a closer look at the necklace. Oliver searched for the path of least resistance to escape the pressing mob. Deborah materialized and guided him through the throng and to the table where the family was gathered.

"Thanks," he offered as air returned to his lungs. He hadn't realized he was holding his breath.

"Not a problem," she said. "Sarah has a ton of friends trying to get her attention. It looked like they wouldn't mind trampling you to get to her."

The adults, a few of the parents of various guests, had congregated in a few tables near the back of the large room. Other tables were filled with chattering and excited teens all dressed to the nines, excited to enjoy an evening just for them. Waiters walked amongst them with trays of alcohol-free drinks or hors d'oeuvres. There were several long sideboards laden with foods, and another table heavy with beautifully wrapped gifts. In the center of it all was Sarah relishing in the attention of her friends. Oliver sat back, satisfied that he had given his daughter the night she deserved.

An attractive woman approached the Copelands' table. "What a wonderful party. Sarah looks so happy," she said.

Oliver could not place her; she was obviously one of the parents, but he did not know her name.

Just as the silence was about to become awkward, Simon spoke up. "Carol Foster, it is so good to see you. Please sit down." Simon looked at Oliver and winked.

Carol sat in a chair between Eileen and Oliver, and moved it closer to Oliver. "Jenna has been looking forward to this night all summer, and I think her brother Austin has as well, but he pretends he doesn't care. We'll be planning Jenna's party soon. I wonder if I might talk to you sometime about it, since you've already gone through the process."

Oliver had done very little planning for the party; that had been Nisha, Mother, and Sarah. "I wasn't much involved, sorry. There are some wonderful party planners in town. They'll be happy to help."

Carol looked disappointed. "Well, thank you again for inviting us. Have a good evening."

Simon laughed and Oliver had no idea what was so funny. "You really are oblivious," his younger brother informed him.

"To what?" Oliver asked peevishly. He didn't appreciate being called oblivious.

"To the women, big brother. Look, here comes Lucy Treadway. She has been trying to get your attention for months. I think she joined Belleshore Community Fellowship just to get to know you better. Why don't you ask her to dance?"

Sure enough moments later Lucy appeared, her caramel colored skin shining and her green eyes sparkling against the deep purple of her gown. Her long, straight hair was held back with a simple but elegant comb. Oliver had to admit that her beauty was breathtaking. Kelly had been beautiful, but she had been cold as well. Oliver stood up. "I'm going to get a plate of food. Does anyone want anything?"

Simon also stood up. "I'll come with you. We need to talk."

Oliver heard Eileen offer Lucy a seat, and the women all started to talk at once. "What is it you want to talk about?"

"You could give her a chance, you know." He put his arm on Oliver to slow his pace.

"I don't have time for a relationship. Besides, how long could any woman put up with me?" Oliver didn't say the rest of what he was thinking. To fully know anyone or let anyone fully know him meant he would have to show her just how broken and weak he was. He couldn't. "I'm saving us both problems by not giving her any hope of dating me. She's gorgeous, so she'll find someone else. Have Denise do her matchmaking thing."

With an exasperated sigh Simon said, "You are clueless. Don't lock yourself away from the world. You deserve to be happy."

"I am happy. Just because everyone else thinks people need starry-eyed relationships doesn't make it true. I'm fine."

"Oliver, you're not happy, and I'm not

fine with that."

The brothers loaded plates with food for the table without further conversation. Oliver wished he could leave the party, but he had promised Sarah he would stay until the end. At the same time, he was glad to have Simon around, so he made a slight concession. "I may not be on-top-of-the-world happy, but maybe I can't be. I am fine. This life is good, and it's mine. I'm as happy as I can be. Sarah needs me. Her happiness means more to me than anything else."

"Oliver, I'll just say one more thing and I'll drop it for now. You take wonderful care of Sarah. She is growing up, and it's time for you to take care of you. Any woman would be happy to have you. Kelly was a sociopath; you didn't deserve what she did to you. Please, don't let her continue to hurt you by making you think you were the problem in that relationship."

They arrived at the table with the food and their personal chat ended as they joined in the family's conversation. Oliver sat down next to Deborah, out of Lucy's way.

13

The fall air was a refreshing balm to Oliver's spirit. It felt good to take his daily walks in the clean, brisk air. The leaves were changing from green to golds, reds, and yellows, painting the world into a love letter from God. Oliver felt an expectancy of things coming to fruition and of family joy. The weather made early autumn his favorite time of year. In fact, he was considering trying another hike with the Levines now that his endurance had increased and the temperature would not torment him.

    Oliver was proud to show off the strolling gardens of Cumberland Manor to Nathan before the grounds were transformed for the Harvest Festival fundraiser put on by the

Arthur Copeland Foundation. "My grandmother grew these roses, and my mother continues to cultivate them. They have won awards and been featured in several gardening magazines through the years. You're lucky to see them still in bloom. Once we have our first frost, it will be June before we see them again."

Nathan was suitably impressed by the velvety deep red flowers. "They are beautiful. I'm not sure I've seen roses so large before. I'm sorry I've missed meeting your mother again."

"She sends her regrets; she is otherwise engaged today." The truth was that she was once again spending the day in bed, too tired to meet anyone. Oliver had become genuinely worried about Catherine's health. She continued to say she was fine, and that her anemia was improving. Although Oliver desperately wanted to believe her, he could see no evidence of any of that. He lied to himself that she was fine, and occasionally even convinced himself of it. If she wasn't fine, how could he be fine? He needed his mother as much as he loved her. Nathan, though, was oblivious to all of this, and Oliver decided that he didn't need to know.

Outside of Deborah and Ash, who were

really more family, Nathan was Oliver's sole friend. Their relationship had begun with business but had grown more personal in the past short months. Nathan, it seemed, needed Oliver. The young man looked up to him as a mentor. Oliver never felt devalued when he was with Nathan. The young man had gone through so much, and Oliver was happy to help him as much as he could. They moved past the rose garden and were now at the entrance of the labyrinth garden. Oliver hated entering it, and in fact, had not done so for several years since becoming lost once in a summer storm. He turned away from it. "Let me show you the Grecian garden. It's just this way."

Nathan followed him along the path. "I'm still unable to access my accounts. It seems whoever stole my wallet has also stolen my identity and, well, it's all just a mess. I don't know how long it's going to be before all of this is untangled. How am I supposed to live? I can't even complete the purchase of the house, much less continue working on it, until everything is worked out."

"I think that it would be more prudent to rent a home for you than to continue living in a hotel. I can rent it under my name and furnish it as well, if you like. In fact, I insist."

"It would be nice to be out of the hotel. But I can't ask that of you."

It was clear to Oliver that Nathan hated to accept what he saw as charity. "You can pay me back when everything is fixed." He enjoyed being able to help a friend. "Let's go look at some places now, shall we?"

"Okay, yes." Nathan relented.

Oliver had become more proficient on his smartphone over the years. He quickly searched the number for the Belle Cay real estate agency and made an appointment. He called Cuthbert to have the car ready for them in twenty minutes, and the two men ambled back to the house without visiting the Grecian garden.

Later that evening, Oliver sat with Catherine as she lay in bed, a game of gin rummy between them. His mother looked pale and emaciated as she leaned back on piles of pillows. Neither mentioned her apparently worsening illness. Oliver dared not acknowledge it. Every time he broached the subject, his mother adamantly denied there was a problem. But each time she said, "I'm fine," it reminded him too much of himself stubbornly uttering the same phrase and hoping people believed him.

Catherine didn't pick up the hand she had been dealt. "Oliver, send Sarah in to me this evening when she gets home, please."

Oliver put his own cards down. "She's going to be home late. It's the last Friday before school starts and the kids are all having a big party. You'll probably be asleep."

"Okay, then send her in first thing in the morning. I barely see her anymore." Catherine was breathing with a great effort.

"Yes, Mother." He poured her a glass of water, unsure what to do for her.

"Robert Song is coming at ten o'clock. I am going to have a meeting with him in the library."

Oliver wasn't sure why he should be frightened by the meeting with her lawyer, but he was. "I can rearrange my schedule and stay here if you'd like."

"No." He could hear the difficulty she had breathing. "It's private, and nothing for you to concern yourself with." She picked up the cards in front of her, laid one down and picked up another.

Oliver followed her lead, and the two played without the extraneous talking that Oliver so disdained. After Catherine won the first hand, Oliver dutifully re-dealt the cards to play again. He adored his mother. She understood him perfectly; there was no need for them to talk, so they could simply enjoy one another.

It surprised him then when she spoke about something that seemed so unimportant. "You've gained some weight. I see some muscle where I haven't for a long time."

"I've been running three mornings a week, and lifting weights three mornings a week. I want my old life back. I want to be me again. I'm up to a mile now, although I've got a long way to go."

Catherine placed her thin cold hand on his arm. "Honey, you are you, and you are amazing, wonderful, and strong."

She would have to say that; he was her son. "I'm not who I was before the accident. I want that life back."

"You imagine your life before as some ideal that it wasn't. Yes, you were an athlete. Yes, you were the smartest young man I have ever known. And you still are that intelligent man. I couldn't be more proud that you've begun to run again. At the same time, you are still you. Your life wasn't any easier then, just different. You had to fight persecutors like Langley Barnett for your position. You had to stand up to me when I wanted you to attend Harvard and you had your heart set on Yale.

You quietly watched Simon be lavished with my attention and favor. And you still didn't hate him or me for it. I think you've forgotten about the bullies you struggled with throughout your middle school years. The way they tormented you. They were the reason you turned to sports. You were just as stubborn and prideful then as you are now. You were just as alone too." Her voice trailed off as exhaustion took her and she closed her eyes.

Oliver sat in silence. He had in fact forgotten about the bullying, or at least about how bad it had been. He had forgotten how he longed to be Simon, who was so easily popular and loved by everyone. He had forgotten how, when his father had died, he had felt like the one person in his corner was gone forever.

Catherine's breathing slowed, and Oliver was about to remove some pillows to let her sleep when she opened her eyes. "Honey, you are so strong and so good. We don't deserve you, but you deserve to be happy. Find a wife and let me know you'll be okay."

Oliver's ever-fluid emotions threatened to break the surface and he fought hard to suppress his tears. He wanted to answer her, but he knew if he did he would cry like the pathetic and damaged man he was. He wanted to tell her he only needed her and Sarah and the rest of the family. But the words were locked behind the tears threatening to break free from his swollen eyes. "I'm fine," was all he managed.

"No…" Catherine drifted off to sleep before she could finish.

Oliver reordered her pillows, put the cards away, and put the chair he had used back in its place. He gently kissed her cheek and rushed off to the privacy of his bedroom. Once there, the dam broke and he wept in safety, alone behind his locked door.

14

Oliver arranged for Deborah and Asher to come stay at Cumberland for the three days he would be in Chicago. Though Sarah would deny it, she needed the supervision that Catherine was presently unable to provide. The three of them would also ensure Catherine was well taken care of and make sure she could enjoy some time with Asha and Daniel as a bonus.

Deborah stood by the door with Oliver as Cuthbert loaded his suitcase into the car. "Don't worry about anything, We've got it. Try to enjoy yourself while you're there. I've heard Chicago has tons of great things to see and do."

"We're staying at The Genevieve. I texted

you, Simon, and Nisha the address. It's only three days." He kissed Sarah goodbye. "I know I don't need to tell you, but please do what Deborah and Ash ask of you, and keep them apprised of your schedule." He hugged Deborah and Asher, then gently hugged and kissed his mother. "Get rest and let Deborah take care of you, please. Deborah, don't let her lift a finger. I'll call you when Nathan and I arrive at the hotel."

"I sure wish we could meet this Nathan," said Ash. "He sounds like a great guy."

Oliver thought Ash sounded more questioning than sincere, like a parent wishing to meet his daughter's untrustworthy boyfriend. He also had not realized until then that Nathan had not yet met anyone besides Simon, and that had been only once. "I think you'll really like him. He'll come to the Harvest Festival. Okay, I need to get going. I'm picking Nathan up before we head to the airport." Oliver got into the back of his car and waved farewell to his family.

The Genevieve was a five-star hotel in a downtown Chicago skyscraper. The hotel boasted that it catered to the businessman, and it offered every amenity the executive might need or want in his 'home away from home.' Nathan had booked a two-bedroom suite rather than two separate rooms, and Oliver supposed he would have to be okay with that. He was unpacking, hanging his suits in the closet, when Nathan walked in to the bedroom without knocking and startled him.

"We have dinner reservations downstairs in an hour, and I thought we could check out a club just two blocks from here afterward. I read about it when I was booking the hotel."

There were times when Nathan's vernacular didn't seem to match the person he said he was. 'Check out' was such a strange phrase to use. Oliver had to remind himself Nathan was more than ten years his junior, fresh out of grad school, and times had changed. Yet something about Nathan nagged at him from time to time. That 'something' was what had kept him from immediately investing in the app. The investment that Nathan requested, and which he promised would make them tens of millions, was two million dollars. Even in light of the loans and gifts Oliver had already given Nathan, that sum was considerable enough to deserve a great deal of deliberation. Oliver knew this trip would help him make that final decision.

"Oliver, does the club after dinner sound good to you?"

Oliver had forgotten to answer him.

"Sorry, yes; that's fine with me." He hoped they wouldn't get back to the hotel too late, since he wanted to work out in the gym before the convention tomorrow.

Oliver called Sarah but only got her voicemail. "Sweetheart, I'm at the hotel. We're in Suite 1525. It's nice, not the St. Regis, but still nice. I'll try calling again after dinner. I love you. Kiss your grandmother for me." He hung up and considered calling Deborah or Asher, but decided against it. He felt out of place in The Genevieve because he didn't know it. The idea of a huge, busy, and unfamiliar city beyond it paralyzed him. At home, he would be finishing dinner at this time, but here it was just now time to dress for dinner. Although Oliver knew he should be famished with the time difference, anxiety had clenched his stomach, and his breathing exercise wasn't helping. A good shower always did the trick, though.

Before stepping into the shower, Oliver examined his body. It was still too slim. He had worked hard and gained twelve and half pounds since beginning his workouts, but couldn't see the evidence. His skin was tanned, at least, since he and Nathan had begun spending many Saturdays at the club pool over summer. He sighed, unhappy with his reflection, and stepped into the shower.

The pressure and heat of the water felt good against his muscles and massaged some of his fear away. By the time Oliver stepped out of the shower, he was at any rate calm enough to feign confidence once again. Dressed in the thick terry robe provided by The Genevieve, he set this evening's clothes out. Sarah, his busy little fashionista, had packed and labeled his tuxedo, suits, and even accessories down to the cuff links, with the days and activities they were meant for. Oliver considered clothes a utility; he only cared about them to the extent that they made him fit in with the occasion at hand. He certainly didn't enjoy picking them out, whether in the store or at home, the way Sarah did.

Nathan did not share Oliver's difficulties with fashion. He was resplendent, dressed in a sharp looking tuxedo, with his gold watch, ebony cufflinks, and designer shoes accentuating his wealth. The two headed down to the restaurant, and Oliver tried to listen as Nathan chattered about the restaurant and the club they would visit afterward.

15

Much to Oliver's chagrin, the club he and Nathan entered pounded with loud music and glared with bright ever-changing and moving lights. The loud music pulsed against his chest and filled his head. While it overloaded his senses and made him want to shrink away, it only seemed to make Nathan come alive. The young man danced as much as walked through the thick crowd to the beat of the hammering music under the undulating lights toward the back of the club. Oliver was grateful for the small reprieve of the VIP section, which was slightly less crowded and where they had a table to themselves.

Although a waitress would come to take their drink orders, Nathan chose to cross the packed dance floor and order drinks from the bar. "I'll be right back!" he shouted to Oliver, who was merely a foot away.

"Yes, okay," said Oliver to no one in particular, as Nathan was well out of hearing range on his way to get drinks. He inhaled for a count of six and exhaled for a count of eight, shutting his eyes to the crushing light display, but opening them again in fear that he would look nervous. It didn't matter how much they had paid to enter the bar; Oliver had no intention of staying longer than it took to finish their drinks.

His heart thumped to the bass, which drowned out any tune he might have heard in the music. The lights and constant movement were bedlam to his mind. It felt as if Nathan had been gone for too long. How long did it take to order two drinks? Finally his friend emerged from the thrashing horde on the dance floor, holding two tall glasses of some neon red and yellow layered concoction. Nathan handed him one glass and took a long drink from the other.

"What is it?" Oliver tried to make himself heard but felt his words fall back on him.

Somehow Nathan had either heard him or otherwise discerned the question. He leaned close to Oliver's ear. "House specialty. It's called a Dragon Fire!" He still had to shout even so close to Oliver. "Listen, I know this isn't your scene, and I didn't realize it would be so loud. Let's leave when we finish these."

"Yes, that sounds good. I'm tired anyway." Appreciative that Nathan knew he didn't enjoy the raucous atmosphere, Oliver relaxed a little and took a long sip of the drink, hoping to finish it quickly. It tasted of sugary cinnamon. He wasn't expecting something so tasty to hit him so hard. Before he knew it, his head was spinning. Maybe he should have eaten a bigger dinner. The noise bothered him a little less, and he took another long drink.

Everything around Oliver slanted, first one way and then the other. He tried to speak to Nathan, to comment on the strength of the drink and ask what was in it, but words would not form. Nathan just stared at him; appearing unconcerned as he watched Oliver try to steady himself in the tipping room.

"I need to go." Oliver hoped he had voiced his thought, since he couldn't hear himself. He stood but the floor moved violently beneath him and he fell down into his chair. Grasping the table, he attempted once more to stand and once more went down.

The bar went bright white, flashed black, and returned to a bright multicolored revolving space. Oliver felt himself leaning heavily on Nathan and being escorted outside. The cold, fresh air hit him, but nothing stopped moving. Even though the blaring noise had quieted, his mind did not clear. It grew foggier and foggier.

"Wait here, I'm getting us a cab." Nathan's voice was distant and tinny.

Oliver tried to ask why they needed a cab to go two blocks, but the thought refused to be voiced. Then everything was thankfully black and silent.

Pain exploded in Oliver's head as he slowly became aware of his surroundings. He could no longer hear the loud music of the bar. The cold and malodorous air was a putrid mixture of urine, rotten meat, sour milk, and body odor. The concrete below him felt like ice. Opening his eyes was more difficult than it should have been. Even though it was dark, the street light above him pierced his slit eyes and sliced into his brain. It was apparent that his face was swollen and bruised. As the rest of his body checked in with his brain, he also discovered that his ribs were possibly cracked, since breathing hurt, and his right ankle was at best sprained. He could not recall how he had been hurt or how he had come to be wherever he was. In fact, where was he? He managed to open his eyes a little wider and looked around him.

He was in a narrow space between two brick buildings, surrounded by piles of garbage. The walls were covered with graffiti he couldn't decipher. Whatever lay beyond the alley remained a mystery. Oliver reached for his phone inside his jacket pocket, but the jacket was gone. Soon he discovered that his phone, wallet, watch, and cufflinks were also missing.

He instantly regretted trying to stand up. His ankle screamed at the attempt, and once he was finally upright, his head spun ferociously. He leaned against the grimy brick wall and slowly made his way to the end of the alley to find out where he was. The building he leaned on was a bar, and next to it was a bodega, but in the depth of the night both were closed. Steam rose from a grate in the sidewalk. Oliver thought he saw a man sleeping on top of the grate. He had no idea where he was; there was no payphone, policeman, or lighted window in sight.

Choosing a direction, Oliver hobbled slowly in search of something or someone.

The sidewalk was strewn with litter and the smell got no better. At last, Oliver saw people, three burly men stood under a streetlamp, talking and smoking. Oliver started to approach them when one looked up,

"What?! What do you want?" He shouted the question with an anger Oliver didn't understand.

He opened his mouth to answer but there were no words available in his foggy brain. Fear told him to keep his head down and walk as quickly as possible away from the men.

"I'm talkin' to you!"

Another of the men spoke up, "Eh let him be, looks like he's already been jumped. Pass me the joint, man."

Oliver tried to walk faster, but his ankle wouldn't cooperate.

The first man yelled again. "I said, I'm talking to you! You show me respect! You're in my hood. I'm the king!" The man was now next to Oliver. He had to be six and half feet tall and at least two feet wide. His skin was chocolate brown, and it glowed beneath the street lamp. His thick hands grabbed Oliver's shirt and pulled him close. Oliver was on the tips of toes under the control of the angry goliath. His face was barely an inch from the man's face, and he involuntarily squirmed from the putrid smell of his breath. "Did you hear me! I'm the king! Get on your knees!"

With that Oliver was pushed down to the cold and dirty sidewalk onto his knees. He looked to the other two men, silently appealing for help, but they stood by laughing.

"That's better," the goliath sneered. "Now give me all your money."

Suddenly there was a gun in Oliver's face. He could see nothing but the black barrel. Frozen with fear, he couldn't even move.

"What are you a 'tard? I said give me your money!"

The gun moved, swung out of sight, and crashed against the side of his face. He tried frantically to answer, to say he had no money, but he was locked inside his own head. The gun and the man had become his entire world.

"Rico! Get his money for him."

A swift kick came out of nowhere, and he landed on his side, the icy cold concrete of the sidewalk smashing his ribs and knocking the air out of his lungs. Rough hands dug through his pants and came up empty.

"He ain't got nothing, Carl."

Carl, the goliath, was only further infuriated, and let out a string of expletives. The gun moved again and crashed down on the top of Oliver's head, sending him once more into blackness

16

Oliver didn't feel like a person. He was just a giant blob of pain crawling through the dense fog. He opened his eyes to the light of morning and feet skirting around him, all connected to people who seemed not to notice him. Could a beaten and unconscious man be so ordinary that he was inconspicuous? He tried to speak, but only a moan escaped his lips. Oliver reached toward a booted foot. It avoided him and stepped further away.

A set of black leather work shoes stopped. One nudged him in his certainly broken ribs. "C'mon, Buddy. Wakey wakey, eggs and bakey! It's time to get up!"

Oliver looked up to see the shoes were

connected to a policeman, and relief flooded him. He tried again to say something, but his words were imprisoned in his brain and his mouth refused to let them out.

"Get up, Buddy. Go sleep it off somewhere else." The police officer reached down and pulled Oliver up by his arms forcing him to stand.

Sharp pain raced from his ankle through his hip. "Help me!" Oliver practically screamed it, but only in his mind. He had not said anything aloud.

The cop pushed him away, "Go on!"

He tried again, desperate to make the words, "Help…" came out in a hoarse whisper.

The policeman finally heard him. He at last looked at Oliver, seeing that he was badly hurt. "Oh, geez! I don't need this." He spoke into the radio he wore on his shoulder. "This is Officer O'Hara; I need an ambulance to the ten thousand block of South Yates."

Oliver couldn't understand the answer which chirped back through the radio. His vision flashed white and black, his head was a whirling dervish, and his muscles could no longer hold him. He collapsed back to the ground and found relief in the arms of unconsciousness.

Everything was too loud. There were too many voices saying too many things at the same time. Oliver tried to open his eyes, but only the right one would obey. The other eye was swollen shut. The lights were too bright, and the one directly over his head flickered and buzzed, making him close his eye against the cacophony and pull a sheet over his face. He tried to imagine where he was. This must be the hospital. He would finally get the help he needed.

"Good, you're awake." A hurried feminine voice came. "How are you feeling? Where does it hurt? How did this happen?"

Oliver tried to decide which question to answer. He lowered the sheet and squinted up to see a thin Hispanic woman in blue scrubs. He slowly sorted through her questions.

She opened his right eye and shone a penlight into it, pressing her fingers against the swollen areas of his face and then pulling the sheet away from him to press her fingers against other parts of his body. "Does this hurt? How about this?"

He was still trying to answer her first questions and now she was tormenting him by pressing into every part of his body that hurt. He groaned in response and tried to pull away, but that hurt worse.

"You don't have ID on you. Were you robbed? Can you tell me what happened?" She asked in the same hurried voice.

Oliver began to sort out what had happened, beginning with getting drunk at the bar. He was about to speak when she interrupted.

"Can you tell me your name? Do you know where you are? Do you know what day it is?" She injected something into the IV line in his left arm. "I'm giving you something for your pain."

Oliver's head became lighter and his pain began to fade. Why did she insist on asking three questions at a time? He was still trying to answer her previous ones. Where was Nathan? Was he alright? Had someone put something in their drinks? He imagined Nathan lying hurt and bleeding, or even dead in the alley where he had awakened after the club. "Nathan…" he rasped.

"Nathan? Nathan what? Listen, Nathan, you've been beaten pretty badly, and we're concerned you might have some internal bleeding. The doctor will be here soon to talk to you. You'll have to undergo some tests. Nathan, can you tell me where you are and what day it is?"

"No…" He tried to tell the nurse he wasn't Nathan, but the effects of whatever she had given him took his voice and replaced his pain with aching exhaustion.

"Nathan, you're in the emergency department. It's Wednesday morning. Get some rest; the doctor will be in to speak with you soon."

How could it be Wednesday? It should be Tuesday, shouldn't it. He drifted off to sleep.

17

Nathan paced from window to door in the hotel room, trying not to throw his cell phone across the room. "It was not supposed to go down like that! You were supposed to rob him and let me come to his rescue, not take him somewhere I couldn't find him. What did you do?"

"Sir, please. Jimmy got carried away. He got spooked by some people passing by and shoved him into the car. We took him to South Deering and dropped him there. Then we was gonna call you and tell you where he was… which we did, but we didn't know he'd be gone."

"If I lost my payout, then you lose yours, too. All you've got is what you pulled off of him. Don't make me do anything you'll regret."

"Mr. Fischer, please."

"What did you call me?" Nathan's fury burst out of him. He grabbed the table lamp, the first thing he saw, and threw it against the hotel room wall. "You had better learn to do exactly what I say, and fast, if you want a single dollar out of me. Listen carefully. I am Mr. Westley to you, and your men will know me only as W. You will say absolutely nothing about me to anyone else on earth. Is there any way that could possibly be clearer to you?" No one was supposed to call him Steve Fischer. Frank was the only one who knew that name, and he had strict orders to call him only Nathan Westley. While neither Westley nor Fischer was his real name, he couldn't risk anyone catching onto the con before he was long gone.

"Sorry, sir, Mr. Westley. I've got eyes and ears on the street and we're looking for him."

"Do not let me down again. Deal with Jimmy or I will deal with you. I want you personally out there looking for the mark! When you find him, take him to the house and keep him there. Call me and I'll figure this mess out." He hung up and threw his phone on the sofa. South Deering was a bad place to be left. He'd be lucky if Oliver weren't already dead. The man could be hurt somewhere and probably lost. Nathan had invested way too much time into this payout to waste on having him die before he wrote the check.

Oliver had just needed something to edge him toward complete trust. Rescuing him from a robbery would have done it. Then that rich son of a bitch would have written the big check, and probably added a nice fat gift, too. He had not been as pliable as Nathan had originally assumed, but as he got to know the man more, getting the smaller amounts had been easy. Nathan had gotten more than $175,000 out of the guy already, plus a cozy place to live. The investment would have been two million. That was nothing to whales like Oliver Copeland.

Nathan needed to calm down. He needed to look like everything was normal, and that meant using the hotel's amenities. He went into the bathroom and carefully put in blue contact lenses, which covered his own light brown eyes. He stared in the mirror at Nathan Westley, got back into character, and went down to the restaurant to eat some of that fancy frou-frou food these fat cats liked so much. He would check out the next day and check in somewhere else as Devon Howard.

18

Simon was worried. No one had heard from Oliver since Monday. The doting father and concerned son had never gone a day without talking to his daughter and his mother, yet he had been silent for several days. That had not been what worried Simon; what did that was the call from Captain Montez that the flight home had been indefinitely delayed and that the call to postpone it had come not from Oliver but Nathan Westley. He had said that they had decided to stay in Chicago for a few more days and refused to say more. Montez knew who his employer was and had called Simon immediately.

Simon had lost count of how many times he had dialed Oliver's number. It went straight to voicemail again. He'd left messages at The Genevieve as well and still had not heard from Oliver. Where could his brother be? Oliver was a grown man, but he had vulnerabilities. Simon's unease was growing as he opened his laptop and pulled up a list of hospitals in Chicago. There were too many for him to call alone. He picked up his phone and dialed his administrative assistant, Arvin. "I'm sorry to call you away from foundation business, but I need help. Meet me at Cumberland Manor as soon as possible."

"Certainly. I'll be there within the hour." Arvin was always so professional.

"Thank you, Arvin, and bring your laptop, please." He then called Deborah and Ash and explained the situation.

Without hesitation, they agreed to come. "We'll be right there. Eileen is here; she'll keep the kids." The worry in Ash's voice confirmed for Simon that he was not overreacting.

Denise was already at Simon's laptop. "Okay, I've divided up the hospitals by area, those closest to The Genevieve and further out in concentric circles. I'll print out a list and we can mark each one off as we call it."

Simon kissed her. "Thank you, darling."

The next call went to Marcus. "Have you

heard from my brother in the last few days?"

"No, Mr. Copeland. He was supposed to be back in the office today, but a Nathan Westley left a message saying he would be out for a few more days. Is there a problem?"

"I'm not really sure. I'm a bit worried, though I'm probably just being protective. Keep things moving there and I'll update you as needed."

"Of course. I'll tell him to call you when I hear from him."

"Thank you." The call disconnected and Simon wondered aloud, "That is two people Oliver should have called who were instead called by Westley. Ollie is not someone who lets other people do things for him, even little things. I thought he was just looking into some investment with this guy, but maybe there's more to it."

"What do you know about him? Do you have his number?" Denise hid her anxiety beneath the busy work of organization.

"I don't, but I'll see if Marcus has it. I met the guy once. I barely remember a thing about him except that he was practically falling over himself to impress Ollie."

He got no answer on Westley's phone and left a message.

Half an hour later Arvin, Simon, Ash, and

Deborah were all making calls to hospitals, while Denise surreptitiously dialed morgues. Two hours passed, and Simon was not sure if he was relieved or more worried that neither Oliver nor a John Doe matching his description was admitted to any hospital in Chicago.

"I guess we need to call the police." Simon felt a fear he had not experienced before. Calling the police meant his brother was missing and probably in danger. Worse than calling the police, he would have to tell his mother and Sarah something as well.

It seemed Denise read his mind. "Call the police, and we'll go talk to Catherine together. When Sarah comes home from school, we'll tell her together as well." She gave him a tight hug and went to search up contact information for the police department.

19

Long hours had passed. Oliver had been subjected to CT scans and X-rays. His cracked ribs and sprained ankle been wrapped. He had a concussion, a gash on his forehead, and multiple contusions, but no internal bleeding.

The doctor was just as quick and harried as the nurse had been. Although he asked questions, he didn't wait for answers. Oliver, try as he might, could not find his voice fast enough to tell them who he was and what he needed. Although it was clear he had been beaten, no police officer, including the one who had called an ambulance, had ever come to take a report. After several hours of observation and tests, he hobbled out of the hospital that afternoon into a city he didn't know.

No matter how he searched his brain, he couldn't remember the name of the hotel where he was staying with Nathan. The name and address, along with all the other phone numbers he needed, were in his phone, and that was gone. His mind was as lost as he was. His thoughts wandered from thought to idea without remembering any of them. Perhaps he should have made someone listen, but each time he considered it, he imagined what they would think of a grown man who couldn't remember the name of his hotel or a single helpful phone number.

Then he saw the payphone, the rare and nearly extinct artifact of the twentieth century was brilliant in the afternoon sun. Oliver reached it, picked up the receiver and listened to the dial tone. "Operator!" he practically cried. But the apathetic dial tone continued. Oliver stared at the phone, utterly baffled by the contraption. Finally regaining some thoughts, he tried pressing various buttons. The dial tone stopped and was replaced with nothing, until after some minutes a buzzing signal replaced it.

Oliver let the receiver drop and walked away, feeling angrier and angrier with each labored step. How could he be so stupid as to not know how to use a phone? Why couldn't his brain work well enough to let him remember how to call the operator and connect with home? He wanted to scream and yell. There was only the slightest amount of resolve left within him to maintain his calm exterior while his insides raged, but it was quickly draining out of him.

People passed him going every which way. Could one of them help? He didn't know and didn't dare ask. Most of them were dingy and tired looking, or dingy and mean looking. He had learned his lesson with the men from the night before. Or had it been longer? He was just as lost to time as he was to position.

Oliver didn't want to keep walking through the terrible pain, but he was an athlete and he trudged forward regardless of the agony. There was no place to stop anyway. Bars and restaurants did not appear as havens but as places where behemoths waited to pounce. "Behemoths don't pounce," he told himself. "You're mixing your metaphors again."

He didn't have the slightest idea how far he went before he finally saw what might be a place to rest. There was a little playground and park on the left. "Thank you, God!" Oliver wasn't sure if he was talking out loud or thinking. He headed for the park, which was not pretty. The playground equipment was decrepit. Trash littered the grounds. Weeds flourished where flowers should have grown.

A fence surrounded the hopeful haven, trying to keep Oliver out. He could go no further; whatever resolve had held his anger in check was gone and rage poured out of him. A wordless scream erupted like hot lava from his throat. He kicked the gate as hard as he could sending fresh agony through his ankle and up his leg. His scream became a loud and long "No!" the single word repeated and he spent his fury and it became despair. He rattled the gate again, unaware of the desperate tears pouring out of him, when it opened. The gate had not been locked, merely closed.

As quickly as the rage had changed to despair, the despair was allayed and became joy. He disregarded every ache and went as quickly as he could to the lone bench next to a dilapidated swing set. The bench's wooden slats could have been a down pillowtop mattress. Sitting down was a reprieve to his entire body. He let out a long sigh and breathed in for six, out for eight. Then, folding his entire length onto the little bench, Oliver closed his eyes. He no longer cared about the ugly broken-down park; rest was all that mattered.

"You were supposed to press the zero to get the operator, dummy!" He would try again when he saw another phone, and hoped he would remember. How worried would his mother be if she didn't hear from him soon? His thoughts raced with new concerns for Catherine and for Sarah. He had to get home. He had to get his brain straight. Oliver continued inhaling for a count of six and exhaling for a count of eight until he fell asleep.

20

Simon knew he had to go to Chicago to talk to the police and look for Oliver. He arranged for Denise and the children to stay on at Cumberland while he was gone. Sarah needed an adult she could count on and Catherine was too weak, Deborah and Ash had gone home that morning and it was unfair to ask them to stay away from their home any longer. Simon also had the daunting task of telling them about Oliver.

Sarah was at school and still blissfully unaware of the situation. Jackson and Kyle were also at school, and Maggie had Cathy and Misha playing outside. Catherine was in her chair in the sitting room, next to the crackling warmth of the fireplace. "Mother,"

Simon said, "I have to talk to you." He set down a cup of hot chocolate she had asked for and sat in the chair next to hers.

"What is it, dear?" She looked so fragile. Her skin was nearly translucent and appeared paper thin. She was gaunt and pale.

Simon took a deep breath. "We haven't heard from Oliver and no one is able to reach him. I'm going to Chicago and talk to the police and look for him."

"You haven't heard from him? What do mean?"

"I'm worried about him. The last anyone heard from him was a message he left for Sarah on Monday to say he'd arrived safely. His phone goes to voicemail. You know, I'm certain he's fine but I just want to make sure." He had yet to convince himself Oliver was fine, but he hoped he was convincing his mother.

Catherine opened her mouth about to speak but instead she gasped and grasped her chest. Her face twisted in pain and then she was unconscious, looking waxy and still in her chair.

"Denise!" Simon frantically called for his wife, but she was already next to him. He feverishly searched for a pulse on his mother.

Denise speedily went into action. He

moved out of her way. "Catherine! Can you hear me?" When there was no response, her sure hands felt for a pulse and she leaned in to listen for breathing. Without turning to Simon, she said, "Help me get to her to floor and then call 911."

He moved his mother, who seemed to weigh nothing, gently to the floor. Denise moved Simon out of the way again, "Call 911 now," she ordered as she began CPR.

The hospital waiting room was too bright. The soft green walls decorated with peaceful paintings did nothing to make it feel anything other than cold. The children were with Eileen and Maggie at Cumberland, and the rest of the family sat in silence, able to do nothing other than pray and wait. The only sound came from Sarah, who sat unabashedly sobbing, wrapped in Deborah's arms. Expressing her emotions was one of the few good things she had gotten from her mother. She had not learned that from the stoic Copelands. Simon had called the police in Chicago and reported his brother missing, and now he waited to hear if his mother would live. He couldn't bear it.

Nisha entered the waiting room carrying cups of coffee, which she set down on the table next to the other paper cups full of cold coffee. "You must need some energy. Please drink this. I am going to go get you some food, and I expect you to eat it. Is there anything at all I can do?" She looked lost, like serving them could help Catherine.

Simon dutifully took a cup of the bitter brew. "You know, maybe some soup from Mitchell's would be good. Thank you, Nisha." He stepped closer to her and quietly added, "Please fax these photos to this number, along with this case number." He handed her two photos of Oliver and the information she would need to send the police department. How could all of this be happening? He felt so helpless.

At long last, a doctor entered the room. The grave looking woman sat down in a chair near the family and addressing Simon who moved to sit next to her. "Your mother has suffered a massive heart attack. The damage is extensive." She paused and looked into Simon's eyes. "She is in a coma and I do not expect her to wake up. I'm sorry. She was being seen by Dr. Nancy Kaplan for end-stage microvascular disease. She should have been on hospice. I will give you Dr. Kaplan's number, and of course I encourage you to get another opinion, but I don't hold out any hope for recovery. Your mother has mere days to live, if not hours. Do you have any questions for me?"

Simon was stunned. He could barely think, much less think of what questions he should ask about news like this. "No. No, thank you," he said very softly. "May we see her?"

"One at a time," she said. "ICU 14"

"Thank you," Simon managed. He wished for the old days of vodka to numb the pain, and then thanked God for the ability to feel it. "Come on, Sarah. Let's go." He helped his crying niece to her feet and led the family to the elevator that would bring them to see his mother.

21

Jimmy walked out of the hospital's emergency room with his arm in a cast, a small price to pay for messing up W's plan to rob the rich guy. He had a prescription for oxycodone in his pocket. He figured he'd sell at least half of 'em to the kids in the neighborhood and make a few bucks. If he wanted to get back in Frank's good graces, though, he needed to find the rich guy. He'd thought Frank was gonna kill him for that screw-up, and it wouldn't take much more to pay that price.

Jimmy thought of himself as a smart guy, so while everyone else looked for the mark without a plan, he used his brain. The mark had probably gone to the hospital, so Jimmy would search all the places near the hospital closest to where they'd left him. Then he'd check out all the places near the next one. With a little luck, and as long as the rich guy hadn't gone to the police, Jimmy was pretty sure he'd find him before anyone else. Jimmy had purposely gone out of his way to South Derry to get his arm set.

He hopped into his Impala. "C'mon, Delilah, take me to the money." He turned the key and pressed the gas. She purred in response. He drove slowly along the path he imagined a person like the rich man might walk. He drove up and down streets looking for the guy. He stopped in diners and bars, took quick looks, and sold a few pills. There was no reason he couldn't pocket a few bucks while looking for Frank's guy, who was really Mr. W's guy. Frank needed him. Everything would be forgiven when he showed up at the house with Mr. Moneybags. Frank would be so happy to have good news for W that he might even give Jimmy a bonus.

Around the corner from Garvey's Pub, Jimmy saw someone sleeping on a bench in a playground. He drove Delilah up slowly to get a closer look and sure enough, it was Mr. Moneybags himself. At least, he hoped it was him. Jimmy parked and jumped out the car. The dude was sleeping on the bench and almost looked homeless, except the black pants and white shirt, though dirty and torn, weren't ratty enough.

Jimmy approached him quietly and took a look to make sure. The guy must've been worked over again. Jimmy, Rory, and Keith had hit him hard a few times, but this fella had been beaten to a pulp. His face was swollen and black and blue, and his left eye and cheek looked like a purple tangerine. Blood was dried on his dirty shirt. His pants were torn at the knees and he had no shoes, just holey socks. His right foot was wrapped in a bandage. "You looked like chipped beef on toast, man," Jimmy murmured, half to himself.

Then Jimmy firmly tapped the guy on the shoulder, "Hey, you can't sleep here. Cops'll grab ya fast. You can't sleep at a playground."

The dupe sat up quickly and winced. He said nothing, just looking at Jimmy with a question in his eyes like he wasn't really awake yet. "You gotta get up from here. Hey, I can help you. I know who you are, and people are looking for ya. Let me take you back to your hotel, what d'ya say?"

The man didn't move. He just looked at Jimmy for a minute, opened his mouth, closed it, and looked again. The fear in his eyes was apparent and it made Jimmy kinda high to know the guy was afraid of him. But he needed to get the guy in the car, so he had to bring the fear down a bit. "Listen, my friend sent me to find you, and he wants me to take you back to the hotel."

Still the man didn't speak. Those drugs must have worked a mess in his brain. Maybe he was on some good stuff from the hospital. Jimmy would roll him before they got to the house and keep his stash for himself. "Are you alright? Can you hear me? Let's get goin'. It's getting cold and I wanna get to happy hour."

As he talked he watched the man and his face as it changed from fear to relief to composure. "The hotel? Thank you. I'm Oliver, and you are?" He stood up, wobbled, and held out his hand.

The guy had transformed from idiot to hoity-toity in a moment. "Yeah, the car's this way." He walked slowly as he watched Oliver's obviously painful totter to the car. He reached out to help him, but the guy refused to lean on him.

They got in the car, and Jimmy talked to make the dude feel safe. "So what happened?."

Oliver didn't answer for about a minute,

he just looked at him. Then he said, "I was robbed, I think, and when I came to I was lost and…"

Jimmy couldn't care less. While Oliver had talked he had gotten the syringe Frank had given him in case he found the target, shoved it into his arm and pushed the plunger.

"and…and…I don't feel…"

The sucker was out. Jimmy was imagining the fanfare he would get for bringing the guy in.

22

Oliver opened his eyes and was completely disoriented. He was on the filthy floor of an even filthier bathroom. The light was off, and the only light came from a window high above him near the bathtub he leaned against. A squeaking sound brought his attention to the corner and the shadow that gained form as he peered into it. A rat was there, nibbling on something. Oliver jerked back and tried to move, but he was handcuffed to the sink between the toilet and tub.

Frozen with fear, he could do nothing more than stare at the fat rodent. In fact, he couldn't take his eyes off it. His mind willed it to stay away from him as it imagined it choosing to abandon its current meal and chew on his toes instead. His fear grew as he watched the rat eat, and he envisioned the multitude of rats that likely lived within the walls coming to taste him.

After some unknown time passed, the rat finished its meal and moved its steely eyes to Oliver. Then it scampered toward him. Oliver jerked back again and an involuntary scream surged out of him. He moved his legs closer to himself, all the while screaming. The bathroom door opened with a bang. A muscular blonde man with a cast on his left arm stood in the doorway. The rat scurried away. But the short feeling of relief was replaced by terror as the angry looking man lumbered toward him.

"You're awake."

Oliver backed himself up as far as possible in the tiny space. The cool of the bathtub pressed against his back.

"Where d'ya think you're going, Mr. High and Mighty? I'll tell ya where, la la land." He pulled a syringe from his pocket and pushed it into Oliver's arm.

Fear dissipated and euphoria replaced it. The blonde man left and closed the door. The sound of a TV came on somewhere beyond Oliver's world. The tiles caught his wandering gaze, and the patterns they made called him in. Random flecks of white on blue became signals that tried to tell him something, but whatever they tried to say, he couldn't understand. Oliver went deeper and deeper into the arrangement of the specks until he melted into the floor.

The brightness of the sunrise caught Oliver unawares. It was becoming a regular occurrence for him to wake up unsure for a moment where he was or what he was doing, and he easily adjusted. The bleachers rose before him and he realized that he was running with the rest of the crew team. His stride effortlessly changed as he mounted the bleachers. The ache of his muscles was exactly as it should be. The world around him shone in high definition. Strauss played in his headphones and Chaz McCandless ran by his side. He hadn't seen Chaz since they were college seniors together. But he must still be a senior if he was running the bleachers.

His friend was talking. "I need help in statistics."

"When is it that I'm supposed to help you, buddy?" Oliver laughed. "With the double down on practice, and my own studying, I don't know when I could help except to take another hour off of sleep."

"I really need the help, and besides, it's easy for you. We can study over breakfast every day. I'll pay you."

"Yeah, okay, breakfast it is. Come prepared and don't pay me, just bring breakfast to my place. I don't eat any of that fast food stuff."

"Thanks, and listen, you need help too." Chaz had stopped running. Stopping would get him extra laps up and down the treacherous stadium seats, but he didn't look concerned about being caught by Coach Denning. Blood ran from his nose, mouth, eyes, and head.

Oliver remembered suddenly and with horror the reason he had not seen Chaz in all these years. "You're dead! You died just before graduation in a car accident."

"You help me ace statistics and I'll help you." The side of Chaz' face was bashed in and blood was covering his track suit.

"I don't need help. I can do anything I have to do. You need help! Let me call the nurse or 911. I have to go call 911. Chaz, sit down."

"You do need help, my friend. I'm fine, but you need help. The truth will set you free." Chaz began running again, leaving a trail of blood behind him.

"I am free!" Oliver shouted to his friend who was no longer there. "I am free!" He tried to run after Chaz but the handcuff kept him in place and pain gripped him. Oliver opened his eyes as the door jolted open again.

"Y'ain't free," said the blonde man, "but W has a plan for you, and hopefully it won't be much longer." Once again the man pulled a syringe from his pocket and injected Oliver with the fluid it held.

As Oliver's brain began to fog over, he seemed to recall that there should be something significant about that letter, but then everything was dark.

23

Jimmy left Mr. Aristocrat crumpled on the floor of the bathroom and returned to the couch to watch TV with Rory and Keith. "He wasn't free, just hallucinating or something. How long you think we have to keep him here?"

"Your guess is as good as mine. How would I know? I only do what Frank tells me to do, and Frank said we have to play babysitter until W tells us the next move. This W guy is a pain in my keister! We do all the hard work and he gets the big payout. What do we end up with except a couple of grand each?"

Jimmy didn't like the way Rory was complaining. He cradled his arm, popped an oxy, and wondered if the place was bugged. "I trust Frank, and a couple a grand for this is better than a lousy couple hundred for a week of hard construction work any day."

Rory shook his head. "You're paranoid, Jimmy. Maybe you need to cut back on the weed. The place isn't bugged."

"I don't think it is!"

"Yes, you do," growled Keith. "You talk about it in your sleep."

"Shut up. I'm watching TV." Jimmy turned the volume up on the television. He liked the channel 7 news because of the gorgeous reporter Jessica D'something-or-other. He didn't really care about what was going on in the city, but Frank had told them to watch the news, so they all watched the news. The boss said it was important to know who was up to what.

Jessica was as stunning, as usual, and at the moment she was reporting in front of the club where they'd snatched Mr. Big Shot. Apparently, he was more of a big shot than Jimmy had known.

A picture of Oliver Copeland was displayed in the corner of the screen while the reporter spoke to the camera. "Oliver Copeland, the CEO of Copeland Enterprises and heir to the Copeland fortune, has been missing since Monday night. He was last seen at the exclusive nightclub Fire and Ice. Police say he is a vulnerable adult, may be confused, and could be in danger."

The anchor broke in. "Jessica, do the police know anything?"

Jimmy thought that was a good question, and he leaned in to hear the answer.

"The police are looking for a person of interest.. They are asking that he come in to answer some questions as they hope to shed some light on the disappearance. If you see Oliver Copeland, police ask that you assist him to the nearest police station or hospital, or call them immediately. The Copeland family is offering a fifty-thousand-dollar reward for his safe return. This is Jessica D'Onofrio reporting at Fire and Ice, Michigan Avenue, Downtown Chicago."

Jimmy stood up and dialed Frank, heading to one of the bedrooms so Rory and Keith couldn't overhear him.

"What!" Frank answered, plainly annoyed at being bothered in the middle of the night.

"I just saw our guest on the news! Police are looking for him, and there's a reward, fifty large. What do you want me to do?"

"Just keep him high, keep him hidden, and wait for instructions. I'll call our friend."

24

Nathan left the police department after a couple of hours of questioning, satisfied that he'd convinced them he knew nothing. He had told them that the last time he'd seen Mr. Copeland was as he left Fire and Ice, but that Nathan himself had been a little bit drunk and a whole lot into a blonde woman he'd spent a while dancing with, so he hadn't seen where Oliver had gone. Nathan told them he had gotten a voicemail the next day from Oliver, saying they would meet up in a few days, but had heard nothing since. The police seemed to believe him when he said he had assumed the other man was just enjoying some R&R in the city. He apologized for erasing the voicemail, but showed the police his call logs, with a few phone calls from Oliver's phone.

Now Nathan was enjoying the crisp cold autumn air and thinking about his next move. He could still rescue Oliver. He would have Jimmy keep shooting him up with dilaudid to keep him docile and suggestible. They would dump him, and Nathan would "find" him and be the hero. Heck, he'd collect the reward the family was offering, plus the investment on his nonexistent smartphone app. He just had to figure out how to make it all happen. But then there was the idea of calling the Copelands for a ransom, too. Two million dollars could easily be ten million with a kidnapping. But those rarely went well, and the police were already involved.

Damn! He wanted to kill Jimmy for this mess. He probably would. A broken arm was too small a price to pay. Frank should have had both his legs broken. If it had been up to Nathan, he would have had Jimmy shot in front of Rory, Keith, and a few of the others. But Frank wasn't hard enough; maybe he was the one who needed his legs broken.

His mind wandered back to kidnapping. Ten million dollars was too good to ignore. The kidnappers always got caught when they gave the victim back or when they tried to pick up the ransom. But there were plans that worked. He could have the money wired to an offshore account, and then route it through accounts in a few other countries that didn't like each other and wouldn't cooperate with an investigation. He knew a thing or two about money laundering, and he could apply those skills to ransom money just as easily.

Once he had the cash, he could kill Oliver and dump the body. He'd give Frank a hundred thousand, and another hundred grand to split between the men, and he'd sail away to the Mediterranean and work his magic on some Plain-Jane rich and lonely spinster. He would marry her and even put up with her for a few years before she met her untimely death. Or maybe he'd just adopt one final identity and live as himself, or whoever he chose to be for a few decades.

He pulled up to the safe house, but knew he couldn't risk going in. He hated coming there. It reminded him too much of his childhood, growing up on Delmar Boulevard in St. Louis as Billy Thompkins. They'd been dirt poor, living on welfare because his mother was schizophrenic and his dad was gone most of the time. He had wanted to be his dad, free to leave whenever his mother screamed at him. She screamed a lot. She would say his dad murdered her parents and that he was a sociopath, or some other crazy stuff, and his dad would take off for a few months or a few years. Billy had been fourteen the last time he had seen the old man. The bastard had set fire to the sofa and walked calmly out the door.

Billy had left at fifteen. He didn't miss either of his parents or sisters and brothers. He had worked some scams, earned bus fare to New York, and become a chameleon, wearing new personalities like hats or coats in order to gain the trust of people he could hustle. A hundred small con jobs had had earned enough money for a real education, the kind that taught him all the other grifts, the kind that taught him how to be anyone he chose to be. Now he lived like a rich man but never paid a cent for anything. He had five identities, and five more ready to go when he retired one. If someone called any of those five names on a city street, he would be instantly in character, but if they called out to Bill Thompkins, they wouldn't get so much as a blink.

Tired of waiting, he dialed Frank's phone. Rather than answer, the man rushed out of the run-down house and got into the car next to him.

"Sorry, sir. I didn't know you were here."

"I don't like being kept waiting. I talked to the police. Keep the mark high. Make sure he doesn't associate Nathan Westley with any of this; that name should never be mentioned. Keep Jimmy as his only other contact. We can send Jimmy down for this if it comes to it."

"What's the plan?' Frank asked hesitantly.

"It's need-to-know. And right now you need to make sure Jimmy, Keith, and Rory are happy and don't plan to squeal for that reward. Throw Keith and Rory a coke party tonight with Selma and Chantal. Make Jimmy keep babysitting, and promise him a promotion while you praise his loyalty."

"Yes, sir." Frank took a bundle of bills from Westley.

"I've got some things to work out, but I want you to meet me in three hours at the Lincoln Street house. Not a word to the guys."

As soon as Frank was out of the car, Nathan left for the comfort of his hotel.

25

Oliver had no idea how long he had drifted in and out of consciousness. It felt like the light through the bathroom window was different every time he opened his eyes. Long enough had passed that the swelling on his face was way down and he could open his left eye now. He was no longer handcuffed, but was still just as much a prisoner in the disgusting cell. He had no idea why he was being kept or what his captors hoped to get out of him. Although he only ever saw the blonde man with the broken arm, he'd heard voices indicating at least two other people, and probably a third, went in and out of the house.

The drugs they gave him always melted

his already shaky ability to think, but it been a while since the last injection, and Oliver was starting to feel lucid again. He hadn't had a clear head in however long it had been since the nightclub. He tried to remain quiet so that he could think freely as long as possible and maybe figure this out.

To Oliver's disappointment, the door opened. The blonde man came into the room, holding a plate in his good hand. "Here. Eat this."

There was a sandwich on the plain white plastic plate. He opened the bread to determine what kind and saw an orange square of plastic-like substance and a greasy brownish circle of something that looked vaguely meaty. "What is it?"

"It's baloney and cheese! What do you think? Eat it or starve. We ain't got lobster thermidor and caviar here."

The food looked the opposite of appetizing but Oliver was starving and took a bite. The taste was hardly palatable but he kept eating. At least he would be close to the toilet if his stomach violently rejected everything. Though Oliver hated small talk, he knew he needed to keep the man here and try and befriend him. "Thank you; I was famished."

The man rolled his eyes. "You're welcome. I ain't your servant."

"No, of course not." Oliver needed to keep the dialogue open. "What's your name? I'm Oliver."

The other man didn't answer right away, but at last he shrugged. "You can call me Jimmy," he said, reaching into his pocket and pulling out a syringe.

Fear gripped Oliver at the sight of it and he wanted to cry. He didn't realize until he spoke that he was crying. "Please! Please don't! I'll be quiet! I'll stay here and not move. You don't have to do that!"

"Yeah, I do. It's orders." Jimmy popped the little plastic cap off the syringe.

Chaz' voice echoed in Oliver's head. *"The truth will set you free."* Oliver had no idea what that meant for him right now, being held prisoner in a disgusting bathroom, but the same voice answered, *"You need help."*

"Please, Jimmy. Those drugs are making me sick. I think they're hurting me." Oliver took a deep breath and knew he needed to share his shame. "Several years ago, I was in an accident, and I came out of it with brain damage. Listen, I have a hard enough time remembering stuff, and I have no idea where I am right now. You don't need the drugs to confuse me. I'm already confused. I probably won't remember your name the next time you tell me, and I have no idea how many times you may have already told me. And I'm afraid. I'm more than afraid. Please don't do this. I think those drugs are hurting me."

Jimmy paused, a look of concern or pity on his face. The needle wavered in his hand, and he looked down at it, as if surprised to find it there. "I'm sorry. I gotta." He bent down to give the injection.

"Please, don't!" Oliver's fear was like a bomb in his chest. His heart was beating so hard he was certain it would blow up and burst out of him. "Can I at least be somewhere other than this bathroom? Please, I'm in so much pain." Oliver was begging. The steady supply of drugs and adrenaline rendered him helpless to control his emotions, and he was crying like a baby and trembling in terror.

"Yeah, okay." Jimmy had cracked. "I'll let you stay in the downstairs bedroom." He reached down to help Oliver up, then pulled him very close. His face was so close that Oliver could smell his rancid breath. "You better not make me regret it."

"Yes, sir," Oliver said, and followed Jimmy down a dark and dusty hallway to a small bedroom, where a threadbare blue blanket covered a little bed. A yellow painted dresser stood against one wall, and a thick green blanket covered a window on the opposite wall. The floor was covered by ugly and colorless carpet. As dirty as the room was, Oliver was grateful that it was not the freezing cold tile of the bathroom.

Jimmy pushed Oliver onto the hard bed. "I will hurt you bad if you try anything!" He jammed the syringe into Oliver's arm and left him alone once more.

The white snow and bright sun on the mountain were blinding, and Oliver couldn't see even a few feet in front of him. He swiftly turned his skis and came to a stop before heading any further down the slope. Though he squinted, the whiteness was the only thing in his vision.

"Why aren't you wearing goggles? Where are they?" Simon stopped next to him, laughing and enjoying the gorgeous day of skiing. "They're around your neck when they should be around your face, big brother. C'mon, wanna race?"

"You bet," said Oliver, pulling the goggles up to his eyes. The sparkling mountain come into focus around him. He saw now the tall evergreens on either side of the steep snow-covered slope and caught sight of Simon a few feet ahead of him.

"Last one to the bottom buys the drinks!" Simon called, pulling further ahead.

Oliver pushed off, and with long strides soon caught up to Simon. In a moment he had passed his younger brother, turning around to look back. "I'll take the most expensive thing on the menu, little brother!"

There was a terrible look on Simon's face. "Stop! Turn, Oliver!"

He turned his head in time to see that the white bright world had turned into a brown tree trunk. He smashed into the tree hard. But though everything should have gone black, it didn't. Instead he was laying in the snow, quite alert and feeling just fine. And while he had never before remembered that last fateful trip down the mountain, he knew that this was it – but with a very different ending. He sat up and Simon caught up to him.

"Oh! No! Someone help, please, someone help! My brother needs help!" He ripped off his glove, dropped his poles and reached into his suit for his phone.

"Simon, it's okay. Look, I'm fine. I don't need any help." Oliver stood up to demonstrate how okay he was.

Simon ignored him and spoke feverishly into the phone to report their position and the situation. He disconnected the phone and slumped over a lump on the ground. "Oh, God! Don't let him die! Oh, my God! It's my fault. Oliver, please be okay!"

Oliver touched his brother's shoulder. "I'm okay, and it was my fault. I wasn't looking where I was going. Rookie move, brother. But I'm fine." He looked to see what it was Simon was crying over. It was a man, broken into a weird position, his goggles smashed, and his face and hair covered in blood. Now Oliver was alarmed too. The man looked dead. "Simon, he needs help! Start CPR! No don't do CPR, don't move him!" When would help arrive? He looked toward the top of the mountain, hoping to see the rescue team coming, but saw no one.

He looked back toward the man, and that was when Oliver saw that it was himself lying lifeless in the snow. Was he dead? Was he a ghost? He fell to his knees beside his own body. "You have to live!"

Simon was still frantic. "It's my fault. I'm so sorry! Why do I make everything a competition? I am so sorry. Please be okay." He looked to the top of the mountain as Oliver himself had just done. "Hurry! My brother needs help!" His grieving brother looked so lost, and Oliver's heart broke for him.

"It wasn't your fault. Simon, is that the burden you've carried all these years? It wasn't your fault. It was all my fault, a stupid mistake. It was an accident. You didn't do this. I'm going to be okay, eventually." He wrapped his arm around Simon's shaking shoulders

Now somehow Simon heard him and looked into his eyes. "You are okay, aren't you? You are better than okay. Why do you think you are so broken and have so much to be ashamed of? This was an accident, and one you worked hard to overcome."

Oliver steeled himself against the tears that begged to be released. Simon's words struck his heart and made him grieve for what his little brother had suffered so quietly. The snow-laden mountain was suddenly gone, and Simon and Oliver stood in the hallway of the rehab center, watching the younger Oliver sitting in a wheelchair and repeating sounds after a speech therapist. That young Oliver had lived with shame over his condition for every moment since he had awakened after the accident. Looking at it all now, he couldn't imagine why he should be ashamed. It was an accident, and after all, he was alive and very well.

"You need help. Oliver, the truth will set you free." Simon's hand was on his shoulder.

"What truth can set me free? I can't even get out of the house! I told the guy the truth and he shot me up! I don't have anything else."

"Keep telling the truth, all of it, and remember, Jesus is the Way, the Truth, and the Life. You have words, you have the Word, and you have love. You need help." Simon turned and walked down the hallway.

Oliver's eyes snapped open and slowly adjusted to the darkness around him. It must have been night. The flat pillow beneath his head was wet, probably with his tears. He pulled the blanket closer around him and closed his eyes to sleep again.

26

Cumberland Manor felt empty despite the many people working, living, and waiting within her boundaries. The feelings of despair and worry only intensified her emptiness as she, like her inhabitants, longed for those gone from the great family. A preternatural quiet hung over all of them. No words were spoken out loud, only whispered. Tension filled the air, a lingering fear that the phone would ring and destroy the tenuous hope the family kept holding.

Henri kept himself busy in the kitchen making a lunch, although he surely knew most of them didn't feel like eating. Charlotte busied herself making the maids schedules. Elsa, Maria, and Daisy each dusted or vacuumed perfunctorily, not speaking of the what-ifs that frightened them. Tom trimmed bushes with half a heart. Irving was in the maintenance shed inventorying the tools, although he could not concentrate and spent the time instead praying for Catherine and Oliver. Cuthbert was in the garage not doing the oil change he had planned to do; he just sat, waiting for the call to either take the family to the hospital or to go pick Oliver up from whatever place he wandered. They and all the rest worked half-heartedly, their minds and prayers on the lady of the house and the first son.

Eileen played with the children outside, and though they didn't know what was happening, the atmosphere kept them subdued and all their games were hushed. Sarah and Deborah sat on either side of Asher in the library, looking through a photo album. Occasionally a quiet comment was uttered by one of them about a picture, but for the most part, they were silent. Simon perched uncomfortably in Catherine's chair at her desk as he and Denise gathered the insurance and legal documents they might soon need. All around the house, soft prayers went up, sparking hope like embers and pushing worries into a corner.

The Manor pined for her magnanimous mistress, the stately lady who was her face and her mouth. Catherine's absence was felt keenly in every person with the great walls. Her missing son was no less mourned; he was the benevolence of the Manor, and even though the family muted their concerns, Cumberland felt them. She was not just a grand house: she was a home, the seat of an honored family. She had cared for them for generations, and she would care for them for many more. She could do nothing more than call out to her family. She reached out her arms in an invitation to summon them home to her. She had undergone pain, sadness, and tragedy with them. She had experienced joy, excitement, and happiness with them, but when all those memories were faded, the love remained. She beckoned her family home to her with all the love the people within her could muster.

27

Simon's hands shook as he tried unsuccessfully to place the documents he and Denise had gathered into a leather portfolio. Denise gently took the papers from him and put them down on the desk. She took his hands in hers and raised them to her mouth to kiss first his left and then his right one. Picking up the pile of documents, she straightened them, slid them into the portfolio, and set it aside. Simon gratefully watched his wife move on to searching for his mother's telephone book, something Catherine had insisted on keeping even though most people stored the information in phones and on computers. He felt so powerless, but Denise was there, the steel in his spine and the solace in his heart.

"Here it is," she said, holding up the neat brown leather book. "Is it up to date, do you think? Should we also print out her contacts from the computer?"

"It's up to date. She writes it all here first, then Nisha enters it into the computer." Simon was drained. He was uncertain how to handle his mother's impending death while also looking for his possibly injured or dead brother. No, Simon thought, Oliver is not dead. He cannot be dead. He's lost, he's hurt, or hopefully just being thoughtless and uncaring, having a good time with a mystery woman. However, Simon knew Oliver would never be so thoughtless. He sank into his mother's chair and put his head down on her desk.

Denise massaged his neck and shoulders. "You spent all night at the hospital sitting with your mother. Go get some sleep or you'll be no help to anyone. The doctors or Nisha will call if there's a change."

He didn't think he could sleep, or even should. "What if… what if she passes before we find Oliver? What if when we find Oliver he's…" He could not voice his fear.

"There's no point in wondering 'what if.' Let's do what we can. For you, that means getting sleep right now. I can give you a mild sedative and you'll wake up in a couple of hours ready to keep going. Allen Kennedy is leading the church in a prayer service right now for both Oliver and Catherine. Asher said he can go to Chicago to investigate things. And police there are doing what they can."

"I don't want a sedative." He got up and went reluctantly to the guest room he and Denise had been staying in.

Denise took off his shoes while he unbuttoned his shirt. He laid his head down on the thick down pillow and fell asleep instantly.

The ringing phone woke Simon from the nightmare he had so often. In the dream, he and Oliver were skiing down the mountain. He tried and tried to stop Oliver from hitting the huge tree but never succeeded. The ringing sounded ominous, and his stomach sunk into his bowels. After a few unsuccessful attempts to answer his cell, he realized it was the landline, and the ringing stopped when somewhere downstairs it was answered. A moment later the intercom in the room crackled to life.

"Mr. Copeland, sir, there is a man on the

telephone who insists on speaking with you about your brother." Ian's voice sounded apologetic.

"Thank you, Ian." Simon grabbed the extension, and with a dread-filled curiosity, he answered, "Hello?" It was more question than greeting.

The voice on the other end spoke in a strangely conversational tone which belied his threatening words. "We have Oliver Copeland. You'll receive a package within the hour with further directions. Do not contact the police or FBI. Talk to no one." The phone clicked and dead air replaced the man's voice.

"Where is Oliver? Is he okay? You'd better not hurt him!" Simon shouted uselessly into the handset. He sat holding the phone, not knowing what to think or what to do. He was so tired. None of this could be real; it just could not be happening. The buzzing signal on the phone finally prompted him to hang up. He put his shoes on and, zombie-like, walked downstairs. How could he tell no one? What was going on?

Elsa was passing him as she headed up for something. "Everyone is in the dining room, eating a little something."

"Thank you, Elsa." He went into the

dining room where the family sat quietly, eating sandwiches and salad only because they knew they had to eat.

Denise saw him and jumped up to make him a plate. "Did you get any sleep?"

"Yes, I think so," he answered taking salad from her. "Thank you."

"Who was on the phone? Is it Catherine?" Asher asked.

"No, it was…I don't know what it was." Simon couldn't say it front of the children. "Kids, go watch a movie. Jackson and Kyle, you know how to put the movie in. Go on."

The children seemed glad to be out of the gloomy atmosphere and left quickly.

When they were gone, Simon described the phone call to the astonished group. "I don't know what this means. Why would someone hold him? What if they're hurting him? I don't know what to do here." He put his head in his hands and longed for a vodka.

Instead, his family gathered around him, and Deborah said, "Let's pray." The group was silent for several minutes as they lifted up their prayers for Oliver, Catherine and for one another. The stillness was broken by the doorbell.

Normally Simon would ignore it and let Ian answer, but now he rushed to the door and opened it to a bland-looking delivery man in a neat green uniform. "Package for Simon Copeland," he said, barely looking up.

"Thank you," Simon took the small manila envelope. "Who sent it?"

"I wouldn't know. Sign here, please." The man held out a tablet and stylus.

Simon signed quickly and closed the door, then examined the envelope. It had only a printed address label and nothing more. Trying not to damage anything which might later be useful for evidence, he picked up the letter opener on the foyer table and carefully opened the package from the wrong end. A small black cellphone slid out. Simon powered it up as he walked back to the dining room and his waiting family.

There was a picture message in the inbox, and Simon tapped on it to see a picture of Oliver, looking drowsy, disheveled, and swollen, and holding that day's copy of the *Chicago Tribune*. The dirt and what could be blood on his torn shirt made panic rise in Simon's gut. He read the attached message aloud. "He is alive for now, and will remain so if you wire ten million dollars to account number following. You have until tomorrow at midnight." There was another message explaining that the transaction would look like: a property sale, filled with details which Simon could not take in at this point. He dropped the phone and sat with a thud in a dining room chair. Denise went to her husband while Deborah grabbed the phone.

"He doesn't look well. My gosh! What are they doing to him?" Deborah handed the phone to Asher.

"We need proof he's okay," Ash said. "I'm texting them back." He typed in his message and pressed send. The air was thick with the tension of unspoken fears and unarticulated thoughts.

The quiet was broken only by Sarah's soft crying and Deborah's futile attempts to comfort her. Simon could not keep his thoughts straight. The photo of Oliver was heart-wrenching: his glazed eyes, his unkempt appearance, and the bloody-looking stains on his shirt meant his brother was not safe.

The ringing of his own cellphone jerked Simon out of his thoughts. The caller ID showed it was Nisha, and his heart sank. Nisha was at the hospital taking her turn sitting with Catherine in the ICU. He answered the phone with trepidation, knowing that although he yearned to hear his mother was awake and well, that was probably not the news Nisha had called to give him.

"Yes! Is mother alright?"

"I'm sorry," said Nisha in her ever calm and quiet voice. "The doctor has said that her pulse, blood pressure and oxygen levels have all decreased, and he suggests the family come and…" Nisha was quiet for a moment and Simon heard her swallow. "Come and say goodbye." Her voice broke and her tears came through. "He said that she probably has just a couple of hours at most. I am so sorry."

Simon was physically and emotionally exhausted, or he had thought he was, but his tears told him there was a deep well of sorrow still within him. He spoke through his own weeping. "Thank you, Nisha. "We'll be there as soon as possible."

He clicked the end call button and looked once more to Deborah's mother, "Eileen, is it too much to ask that you stay with the children?"

"Of course not. Please tell Catherine I love her. I'm so sorry." She hugged Simon.

Denise spoke up, sensing his need to alleviate just a bit of the burden of leadership "I think we can take Oliver's car and driver. I don't feel up to driving. I doubt any of us do." She dialed Cuthbert's number and spoke quietly into the phone.

"Yes." Simon didn't want to make any

more choices; there were too many terrible decisions ahead of him. He looked at the uneaten sandwich on Sarah's plate, took it as well as her napkin, and handed it to the forlorn teen. "Your dad and your grandmother wouldn't want you sick on their accounts. We need you."

"Okay. I'll eat it." She took a bite and walked toward the front drive of the house.

"Mom," Deborah said, "There are bottles and baby food in the fridge for Daniel. He likes the finger foods, so I have them ready for him in the blue containers, and you supplement with the vegetables in the orange containers."

"I know, dear," said Eileen as she kissed her daughter's cheek. "Go, we're all okay here." She took Daniel from her daughter's arms.

The group remained quiet as they gathered their things and distractedly put on their coats. Simon ushered each of them to the front door to wait for the car. Cuthbert must have been waiting and ready for the call, because he was pulling up as they stepped out. Motioning for the driver to stay where he was, Simon opened the door and watched each of the people who so loved his mother get into the car to say goodbye to her. He stepped in last, closed the door, and wished there were something he could do.

28

Simon sat amongst the machines and IV poles surrounding his mother, who somehow appeared tiny in the hospital bed. He put her cold, limp hand in his own, and pressed it firmly as he tried to imbue her with his warmth and his life. She didn't look like Catherine Copeland lying there; she was a shadow of the magnificent woman who was his mother, the queen of Belle Cay, the altruistic benefactor to the poor, and the consummate lady to whom the rest of the wealthy looked. "Mother, I'm not ready to say goodbye. How can I?" His tears fell unchecked as he lifted her hand to his mouth and kissed it. "Please, please stay with us. I know you're ready to go home. You want to be with Jesus face to face, and you want to see dad again. Who could blame you? But I'm not ready for you to go. We prayed, we prayed for your healing but God told me, that your healing will be in Heaven with Him. So, I have to let you go.

"But maybe you could hang on for just a little while. Oliver should get to say goodbye too. I'm doing everything I can to bring him home to you, Mother. I won't stop until he's home." Simon's voice broke as he felt himself break under the weight of all that was happening. "I don't think I can do this," he cried. "God help me. Please show me the way to go. Lord, I am so lost. I was never the strong one, and now everyone is looking to me for strength. Be my strength, Father." He had no more words to pray, so he put his head down on his mother's chest and cried as he listened to the slow beating of her heart. The tears stopped and peace filled him with each beat. He closed his eyes and breathed, willing his mother's respirations to match his own and willing her heart to keep a steady beat. Even as he tried to make her heart keep beating, he listened to it slow, skip a beat, and slow again. He squeezed her hand, trying somehow to keep tell her heart going. The beat of her once stalwart heart could not maintain a steady rhythm.

Suddenly, Simon felt the pain it had to be for her to continue. He understood the struggle she went through. He couldn't ask her to stay any longer. It wasn't fair. He whispered to her, "It's okay, Mother. Let go. I will bring Oliver back, and he will say his goodbyes then. Go home." The arrhythmic beat slowed and the came to a stop. A sigh released itself from her mouth and Simon knew that the formidable Catherine Copeland was gone.

29

The bedroom door swung open, bringing Oliver out of the haze inflicted on him. He jerked into a sitting position and thought, "I can do all things through Him who strengthens me." He didn't know why he was being held or what his future had in store. Fear had become almost tangible; he could almost see his death, like a monster looming in the dusty shadows of the room that had become his dungeon. Panic tried to overtake him, but he inhaled for a count of six and exhaled for a count of eight to keep it at bay. He looked around and tried to gain his bearings.

Jimmy held the plate in his hand and a 2-liter bottle of soda in the crook of his good arm. Oliver eyed the baloney and cheese sandwich hungrily. Without his routine, he couldn't track time and wasn't sure how often he was getting food, but he knew it must have been a long time if he'd begun craving the strange baloney and cheese, the only food Jimmy ever brought.

Jimmy set the plate and bottle down on the bedside table. "Eat up."

Oliver snatched the meal and ate it voraciously while Jimmy watched. "Thank you. Thank you, Jimmy." He wished for a napkin, but that wasn't something Jimmy thought of. He was very thirsty, and while sugary colas normally would never have been his choice, he wanted the soda badly. There was no glass, just the giant bottle. He picked it up but couldn't loosen the lid to get to the liquid inside. He was too weak, or maybe still too out of it from the constant injections. "Jimmy, can you please help me? I can't do it." What had happened to his pride? Was he more broken now than before?

Despite his broken arm, Jimmy had no problem opening the bottle. With a look of pity, he handed Oliver the soda. "You gotta stay hydrated."

"Thank you. You know, Jimmy, you're taking really good care of me. I appreciate it."

"Don't bother. It's my job. You're my job. C'mon, you gotta piss now. Don't try nothing."

Oliver got up from the bed, his head swimming and his legs wobbling. "I won't. I promise." He obediently followed Jimmy into the bathroom across the hall.

Once back in the bedroom, Oliver wanted to put off the injection for as long as possible and perhaps keep Jimmy with him. He had not understood how lonely forced solitude could be. "I know you're mostly by yourself here. Maybe you want to play some cards or something. I could use some company. I normally play cards each night with my mother. She's the real card player. I lose more than I win."

Jimmy said nothing, but he didn't move either.

Hope fluttered its wings in Oliver's chest. "I'm worried about her. She's ill, and I probably shouldn't have taken this trip, except she insisted I go. I wish I could call her and tell her I'm alright, and tell her what a good guy you are."

"I'm not a good guy," Jimmy said flatly.

"Yes, you are! I hear you talking sometimes. You were the one who convinced the others I would be okay in the bedroom.

You bring me food and soda when you could let me starve. I've heard you stand up to them. You're loyal to your employer. Maybe you are doing some things that aren't so good, but, well, no one's perfect. We've all done bad stuff. There's hope for you, Jimmy." Oliver felt frenetic. He was not certain if it was the drugs, or fear, or a combination of both. It was as if his brain and his heart were racing down a mountainside, speeding away and leaving his stomach behind to be sick.

"Yeah, there's hope. I'm getting a nice paycheck for you, and I love my mother too. I'm gonna be able to pay her rent for a few more months because I'm doing my job."

"You pay your mother's rent? That is good. Not many people care so much." Oliver washed his hands and dried them on an ugly towel that probably made his hands as dirty as they were before he washed them.

"My mom's the best," Jimmy answered. "She worked three jobs most of the time while I was growing up. My dad was a deadbeat. Now I take care of her. She works one job; she's a waitress at Finnegan's."

Oliver's hopes were lifted. "Your mother sounds like a good woman," he said, following Jimmy back to the bedroom.

Jimmy sat down on the bed next to

Oliver, "She is. She raised me good. She thinks I work construction. I don't tell her how I make money. It's not her fault I didn't follow her rules. You can't make enough money to survive doing something like construction. You wouldn't understand how important money is." Jimmy leaned forward about to stand.

Oliver needed the company, and he didn't want Jimmy to leave. "You're right. I've never had to think about money. I'm blessed. It's rare, and maybe even not fair. But I do know about wanting to please my mother and take care of her. My mother must be worried sick about me. She wasn't well when I left for my trip. She worries about me more than she should."

Jimmy sat back down on the bed. "Why should she worry? Aren't you a big shot filthy rich executive, a fat cat and all that?"

"I am successful, but I think I mentioned something about my accident. Did I? I don't remember. I was in a skiing accident, and it left me with brain damage." Oliver knew he had to bare everything to gain Jimmy's trust.

"You mentioned it, but you don't look or sound retarded to me."

Oliver winced under the weight of the derisive term. "I hide my limitations pretty well. I've learned to cope and I've learned to pretend. I'm not..." He swallowed his disgust for the word. "I'm not retarded. I have some cognitive impairments. I have memory problems. My emotions are all over the place. I never know how I'm going to respond to something, sort of like a toddler who can't control his feelings yet." He hated telling this stuff to Jimmy. It felt he was opening a door and letting Jimmy see the pathetic creature he was hiding behind it.

"Well, man, you're awfully good at it, cause I sure can't tell you're cog... cog-whatever. I don't see no impairments."

"Thanks. I'm worried what the drugs are doing to me, though. I can't think at all and I always feel foggy."

"I'm following orders," Jimmy shrugged. "Good news for you is, I've been ordered to hold it for a couple of hours. But if you give me any problem at all, you'll regret it."

"There won't be a problem."

"Good." Jimmy took the empty plate from the bedside and left the room.

Oliver heard the lock of the door and was alone again. Finally awake, and with the fog lifting from his brain, he prayed.

30

W had told Frank exactly what to expect and do. Sure enough, he got a text from Copeland asking for proof of life. Frank was already at the house filling Jimmy in on the plan when the message came through. They had decided to let him come down from his high so he could make a nice little video, and then they would pump him full of whatever drugs would keep him docile. The mark's regular dose had been withheld, and he should be able to perform pretty well now. "Jimmy, c'mon; it's time to make a video."

Jimmy grabbed the phone and obediently entered the bedroom where they were holding their hostage.

Frank put a mask on his face and walked

in behind Jimmy. The guy on the bed jumped at the sight of him; the clown mask was appropriately frightening. Frank shoved a typewritten paper into the guy's shaking hands. "Read this! When I say action, say it into the camera! You better be convincing. Earn an Oscar!"

The guy moved his eyes slowly over the page and didn't speak. His hands shook violently. Frank was about to smack him when he finally said, "Okay," in a voice so quiet and trembling that Frank nearly couldn't hear.

"Make sure you say it loud and clear!" He pointed to Jimmy. "Alright, start!"

Frank stood next to the guy, gathering all of himself to appear as imposing as he could. Pulling a gun from the back of his pants, he poked their mark hard on the shoulder and stood pointing it at him.

The guy didn't say anything. He just reread the page in his quivering hands.

This time Frank hit him hard across the face. Blood flowed from their captive's nose. He drew his breath in sharply, probably got a lungful of blood, and began coughing. When the fit stopped, he looked at the lens of the phone and said, "I'm okay for now, but if you don't send the money, I'm dead." Blood dripped from his nose into his mouth, making the dude cough again.

Frank didn't immediately cue Jimmy to stop filming. Like a director, he chose to get a bigger picture of the seriousness of the situation. Copeland's coughs turned to choking, and Frank moved the gun across his throat to end the video. "Geez! Make sure he doesn't die just yet, Jimmy." He grabbed the phone and left the room.

The video was everything he hoped it would be. Frank laughed as he pressed send. Jimmy was out of the room now, holding a bloody towel. "How much you think W is getting for the guy?"

I dunno. Ain't my business." Jimmy walked briskly away.

Frank followed him and watched him toss the towel in the laundry. "I think he's getting a cool million at least. Our share's gonna be nice."

"Yeah." Jimmy wasn't too talkative.

"You're boring me. Go dose the guy, I'll see you later." Frank was on his way to get some other business done. Cherri was waiting for him at home.

31

Oliver kept the towel pressed over his nose, trying not to check whether the bleeding had stopped. A voice kept telling him that he was going to die no matter what. Whatever the ransom, his family would pay it, but these men would kill him in any case. He told the voice to shut up. He was befriending Jimmy, and somehow he would find a way out.

He prayed, "God, help me! Set me free. Show me the way." Though much of his prayer was wordless, he knew God heard him.

The truth will set you free. I am the way.

Oliver knew it was true. He wasn't certain yet how, but he would keep talking to Jimmy, and by some means, he would be free. He took the towel off his face and examined it.

There was no fresh blood. His fingers felt his throbbing face and relief broke through his dread when he found no swelling. At least his nose wasn't broken. "I can do all things through Him that strengthens me," he thought. He knew that verse wasn't about being a superman. It was about handling circumstances the way Jesus would, regardless how good or bad they were. He folded the towel and set it on the floor near the bed.

Outside the room, he heard the TV click on, and did his best to eavesdrop on the nightly news. It gave his mind something to think about besides his imprisonment. What was happening at home? How were his mother and Sarah? Sarah was probably terrified. She must feel so alone. Oliver longed to hold Sarah in his arms and tell her it would be alright. Simon, Denise, and Deborah would be there for her, but they were not her father. He was, and he and Sarah needed one another. They were a team. Since Kelly had left, the two of them had been inseparable. Even before Oliver's ex-wife had gone, they had filled in the spaces Kelly had not been able to fill. What would Sarah do if he were gone too? These men would not win. They couldn't. Oliver would get out of this hole somehow. He had no idea how long he had, but he knew he had to make a move soon.

The sound from the TV caught his attention as he heard his name mentioned. "The family has made no comment, but it is believed that stress related to Oliver Copeland's disappearance may have contributed to a heart attack. One source reports that Catherine Copeland had been ill for months, and she had not been seen publicly since July. The family's attorney, Robert Song, would say only that she died surrounded by family. Oliver Copeland remains missing, and the police report no new leads."

It took a moment for the news to sink into his brain and explode. The world became a red blur. The only sound was the "Noooooo! No! No! Mother! No!" that poured from his soul. His rage knew no words and his fury no sense. Pain welled up from deep within him and searched for expression. His hands found a half-emptied soda bottled and threw it against the wall before grabbing the lamp and crashing it against the door. His wails continued as he released the wrath he had locked away for years. He felt nothing but anger as his fist hit the door over and over. The door swung open as Oliver's adrenaline enhanced punches broke the flimsy lock, but he couldn't see it through the storm of emotion that poured out of him.

32

Jimmy was up instantly at the terrible wails coming from Oliver's room. He raced to the room as the door pitched open before him. Inside, Oliver was punching the wall and howling. The distraught man did not react as Jimmy passed the open door to try and stop him. Jimmy grabbed him from behind, pinning Oliver's arms to his body and wrestling him to the ground. Jimmy held him tightly until Oliver at last seemed spent.

He didn't let go as Oliver's screams turned to moans and finally words cried in agonizing grief. "Mother…No, mother…no."

When Oliver went limp, Jimmy released his grip. Oliver melted down onto the floor and curled himself into a ball. The adrenaline that had made Jimmy act was now used up, and genuine concern for Oliver replaced it. He had no idea if Oliver could hear him, or was even aware of his surroundings. "I'm sorry about your mom." He didn't really know what else to say. "Here. Come on and get in the bed."

Whether or not Oliver heard or understood, he compliantly got to his feet and walked zombie-like to the bed. Jimmy pulled the blankets down. "Get in. It'll be alright. Get some sleep." Oliver got into the bed and turned his face away from Jimmy.

There was a ready syringe in the kit in the living room, which Jimmy left to retrieve, eyeballing the broken door as he returned with the needle in his hand. "What am I gonna do about that door?" he asked himself. "I guess I'll have to move him to my room. That should be fun." Oliver was now sitting up in the bed, breathing heavily and repeating "Mother, mother" in a seething voice.

Jimmy was really scared now, not for himself, but for Oliver; he wasn't sure the man would be okay again. "I'm sorry," he said sitting next to Oliver. "Lay down. Get some sleep."

"It's my fault. She died because she was worried for me. I killed my mother." Oliver looked around the room at the mess, then got out of the bed and started picking up the debris. "I'm sorry. I lost it. I told you I couldn't control myself." He winced and looked at his bloody hand. "Oh, God! My mother is gone." He dropped the shards of ceramic from the broken lamp and stood weeping.

Jimmy was at a loss. It wasn't Oliver who had killed his mother. It was him, and Frank, and W. "I'm gonna get some ice for your hand. I'll be right back." He no longer cared what Frank or W had to say; he wasn't dosing the guy anymore. He wasn't even sure he wanted to be a part of this. No amount of money was worth killing someone's mother. Besides, if Oliver's mom had died from stress and grief, how did they know Oliver wouldn't be next?

33

Oliver held a plastic bag of ice to his aching hand and wept for his mother and for Sarah. What would they do without the great Catherine Copeland? Sarah would be devastated. All the children would be upset, but especially Sarah, who was so close to her grandmother. Looking around at the wrecked remnants of the room, Oliver could hardly believe he had done all that.

Jimmy stayed next to him. "Man, I'm really sorry."

"Thank you," said Oliver. "She was sick for some time, more sick than she let on. I'm okay though, Jimmy. I'm sorry about this." He pointed to the broken lamp, the soda stained wall, and the rest of the mess he had made.

"Dude, it's fine. I love my mom too, I'd have freaked out if I was in your place."

"Freaked out," Oliver chuckled. "That's fitting. I did freak out. But not now. I'm dreadfully sad, but I'm also happy for my mother."

Jimmy looked bewildered. "Happy for her?"

"Yes. She's gone home to be with Jesus. I'll see her again one day."

"You'll see her again. Okay." Jimmy spoke the words slowly as if to a child who believed in fairies.

"I will. One day, Jesus is coming back and when He does, every person who has died will be brought back to life. All the people who believed in Jesus and accepted His salvation will be with Him forever. Anyone who didn't will face judgment for all the wrongs they've done."

Jimmy snorted. "There ain't no hope for me, man. I gotta have all sorts of judgment coming."

"We've all done too much wrong to go to heaven," Oliver told him softly. "Jesus died on the cross to pay the price for all our wrongs, and He rose from the dead so we could live with Him eternally. You only have to believe it, give your life to Him, and say it. You don't have to make up for all the wrongs you've done. He already paid for them."

"What does that mean, give your life to Jesus?"

"It means you make Him your boss. You take orders from him and you do what he says, just like you're doing with Frank now. But Jesus is a good master. He's all love. He helps you to be a better person, and to make other people happier, too."

Jimmy sat contemplating for a minute. "That sounds better than...this." His eyes drifted around the shabby room and the debris on the floor. "But the stuff I've done...."

Oliver could see almost see the guilt weighing down on Jimmy's shoulders. "Jesus already knows it all," Oliver insisted. "If you tell Jesus how sorry you are and if you choose not to do those things anymore, He forgives completely. He pardons you, and you are free, no longer condemned to hell. He forgives so completely that when God looks at you, He sees only Jesus' goodness. He loves you so much, Jimmy!"

Oliver could tell that Jimmy was interested, but that a lot of the things Oliver was saying made no sense to him. "Yeah? I am sorry. Sorry for all of it. But there's so much." Jimmy stood up. "I'll be right back." He walked out of the bedroom and the left the door open.

34

Horror grew like a weed, trying to choke out Simon's hope as he watched the kidnapper's video for the third time. This time he had Denise, Deborah, and Asher watching it as well. Whatever the kidnapper imagined, gathering and wiring ten million dollars was no small feat, particularly the day after one's mother has died. But he knew he had to do it if there was even the smallest chance that Oliver could be saved. "I think we need to call Robert Song. As the family attorney, he can tell us just how to do this."

Deborah was weeping. "Oh, Lord!" she cried, and hid her head in Asher's chest.

Asher didn't hesitate to pray. "Father, show us the way. Bring Oliver home to us. In

Jesus' name, we pray. Amen."

Three quiet amens echoed his. Every time Simon closed his eyes, he saw the man with the clown mask smashing Oliver's nose. He saw his brother crumpled and broken in the snow, this time dead, because he knew that regardless of the ransom, the man or men who held him would kill Oliver. "We can't let this happen! Denise, will you please call Mr. Song? I'm calling the police. We have to find Oliver before midnight."

Denise wiped her red eyes. "Yes. And Simon, you are not alone in this. We're all here with you." She took his hands in hers and kissed him before going to make the call.

Two hours later the house was abuzz with activity. Simon had moved Eileen, Sarah, and the children to Copeland Gardens with a police escort who would also stay with them. The police had contacted the FBI, who had taken over the library with people and equipment. He sat bewildered by everything as Agent Greene spoke.

"We'll work with the bank so that you can send the money, but you will not send it until 23:59. I want you to try and make contact with them. Tell them you want to talk to Oliver live. We'll do our best to find his location that way." The slim brown-haired man spoke with confidence, plainly trying to allay Simon's fear.

Pulling out the cellphone he had received from the kidnappers, Simon said, "I'll do whatever you tell me to do." He spoke aloud as he typed the text into the phone: "I want to talk to Oliver."

"Now we wait," said the agent. "If and when they call, wait for my signal to answer."

"Yes, okay." Simon was so weary. He ought to be planning his mother's memorial with his brother, not trying desperately to save his brother's life.

Elsa entered the room. "Mrs. Copeland told me to bring tea, coffee, and sandwiches for everyone. She said to make sure you eat something, please, Mr. Copeland."

He took a sandwich from the tray and ate it mechanically, unaware of what he was doing. Watching her serve each of the grateful agents in the room, he envied her for having something to do. There was nothing he could do now expect wait. He couldn't write a eulogy or talk to funeral home, and his mind was exhausted with thoughts of Oliver missing somewhere and bleeding into the snow.

"Excuse me, Mr. Copeland." Ian stood at

the door of the library. "The pastor is here."

Thankful for a reason to leave the busy room and glad to have Allen Kennedy to help, Simon took his sandwich and a cup of coffee. "I'll meet him in the sitting room with the rest of the family."

"Yes, sir," replied the butler, who disappeared ahead of Simon.

Allen's salt-and-pepper hair, compassionate eyes, and comforting arms greeted Simon and lifted a heavy weight off his shoulders. "Simon, I can't even imagine what you are all going through right now. I loved Catherine so very much. I would like the honor of planning her memorial."

"Thank you, Allen," Denise said, her relief almost visible.

"Yes, that means so much. She wrote out her wishes. I'll go get them for you." Simon started to leave the room.

"No," said Asher. "You stay. I'll bring the portfolio down. It's on her desk, right?"

"That's right. Thank you so much." Simon sat down, feeling a reprieve from the burden he now realized he was not carrying alone.

"Now," said Allen, "we'll pray, and I am here to listen and do whatever it is you need. I have many people in the church chomping at the bit to help in any way they can. I have only to ask and it will be done." The pastor's southern roots came through when he spoke, and often the colloquialisms brought smiles and even laughs. Today, though, Allen's vernacular brought an unexpected peace to Simon.

As Allen prayed, Simon was filled with confidence in God. His faith grew and pushed his anxiety out. "There's nothing more I can do," he thought. "But I just know that God is going to bring Oliver home. He is taking care of Oliver, and He will do it."

35

The bedroom door was open. It would be a simple matter to walk out and be closer to freedom. Oliver knew he could try to escape, and he would probably succeed. It was God who had left the door open, not Jimmy. They had formed a tenuous trust with one another. However, if he escaped, he knew Jimmy would pay the price for it, possibly with his life. There was no way Oliver would have a willful part in ending someone's life, or even hurting them.

There was a caring spirit within his captor. Oliver had seen his reluctance in injecting the drugs, and felt the concern Jimmy had shown for him. Oliver had awakened once to find himself covered with a thick blanket in the frigid room, and he knew who must have done it. He knew too that Jimmy was on the brink of a decision for Christ. Jimmy's eternity, his salvation, was more important to Oliver than his own freedom. So he stayed where he was, on the bed, holding ice to his throbbing hand.

"Lord," Oliver prayed, "Soften Jimmy's heart. Open his eyes and let him see and understand how much you love him. Call him and keep calling until he answers with a yes. Thank you for making him the one who took care of me here. I know that you have me in your hands, and I know you have Jimmy. Bless him and bring him to you. In Jesus' name, amen."

He opened his eyes to see Jimmy standing in the doorway. "You thanked God for me? You asked Him to bless me?" He stood there staring at Oliver for several moments, plainly not understanding what had just happened. "But I kept you locked up and drugged you. I helped kidnap you. How could you do that?"

"I'm glad it was you, because I can see that you care about people. You kept me alive, and you heard me when I needed something from you. Believe it or not Jimmy, I love you. I love you because Jesus loves you, and because God created you. We did not meet by accident. I've been praying for you and for whoever kept me here."

"Jesus loves me." Jimmy was silent for a few moments. "My mother has been telling me that for years. I've always just thought it was her way of trying to get me to behave. Gotta do the right thing cause Jesus is watching." He looked up. "You know I'm a bad guy and you still think He loves me?"

"I know He does."

"You said that I just have to say I'm sorry, stop doing the bad stuff, and give Jesus my life. Tell me how to do that." Jimmy looked back over his shoulder, then at Oliver again. "I don't care what Jesus tells me to do. It's got to be better than this."

"The Bible says all you have to do is confess that Jesus is Lord, which means he gets to be in charge of your choices from now on. You have to believe that He was a real person, who really died on a cross for your sin and then rose from the dead, and that He is the Son of God. It is that simple. He takes care of the rest. He makes you a whole new person, a person who, when God looks at you, sees you as good."

"I do believe it," Jimmy said forcefully. "I mean it. All that stuff my mom taught me, that Jesus died on the cross for my sins, I didn't get it then, but I get it now. He died and He came to life again. I believe it. I am giving Him my life from this moment on." Jimmy turned around. "That means I have something I have to do. Be back in a few."

Oliver remained on the bed, stunned and thrilled. He laughed and prayed again, "Thank you, Father! Thank you! You are so good!" He stood up and walked around the room, picking up pieces of the mess he had made before, and dropped them and the ice bag into the trash can. He sang out the tune of *Ode to Joy* and felt his soul soar uninhibited.

Jimmy re-entered the room. "I called the police, I turned myself in, and the rest of 'em too. Frank, Rory, and Keith. There's someone else, too, the guy in charge of it all. I only know him as W, but I think the police can find him too."

Oliver was astounded. "You..." What could he say? There didn't seem to be anything, so Oliver just stared at him in disbelief for what seemed like hours. "Thank you, Jimmy," he managed at last.

"I think we need to go to the front lawn and put our hands up. It might be scary, ya know? They'll take us both until they get the whole picture. I'm gonna tell them everything."

The two walked through the little house. Oliver gazed around at the thrift store mismatched furniture covered in dust, the empty beer cans, and the other debris littering the place. Then, as Jimmy opened the door, the bright afternoon sun burst in. Oliver stepped outside. The brisk air filled his lungs and the sun shone upon the world, making everything glitter. Police sirens echoed off the run-down buildings, becoming louder by the second, until the attached cars came to a stop in front of him and brought a momentary quiet.

Policemen jumped from the three cars with guns in hand. One shouted, "Down on your knees! Hands up!"

Oliver obeyed, and it seemed instantaneously he was painfully handcuffed.

The officer behind him shouted, "What's your name? Tell me what's going on here!"

The same thing was happening to Jimmy a few feet away, but Oliver was not able to hear what Jimmy answered. Jimmy was brought to his feet and put in the back seat of a cruiser.

Fear threatened to keep Oliver's mouth closed, but he breathed a prayer and said, "I'm Oliver Copeland. I've been kept prisoner here, for... I don't know how long."

Another officer came away from where

Jimmy was in the back of the police car and said, "According to the other guy, this is the missing millionaire Oliver Copeland. He was kept against his will. Officer Denton, go ahead and take the cuffs off of him." The dark-haired woman addressed Oliver. "Mr. Copeland, we're going to take you to the police station and talk for a while, then hopefully get you back home."

The cuffs came off and Oliver brought his hands back around to his front. Standing up was not so easy. He only now realized how exhausted he felt. Still dizzy from drugs and weak from the ordeal, Oliver took Officer Denton's hand, stood and followed him to a car.

36

The ringing phone made Simon run into the library to answer just as the FBI had explained he ought to. But it was not the cell from the kidnappers. It was the house phone. Agent Greene signaled the go-ahead and pressed a button as Simon lifted the receiver. He prayed silently and said, "Hello, this is Simon Copeland."

"This is Captain Redding of the Chicago Police Department." The voice was deep and smooth, reminding Simon of James Earl Jones. "Your brother is safe. He is at the hospital, the Rush University Medical Center. He's being checked out to make sure he's okay."

Although the man continued speaking

Simon didn't hear what he said. Joy filled him and thrust fear away. Agent Greene was writing out the details he would need to reunite with his brother. According to the captain, Oliver had somehow talked his kidnapper into turning himself in, and the man was cooperating fully. The police had three other men in custody and were looking for one more, someone in charge of the operation.

Cheers rang through the house. Simon, who had been certain that he had no tears left within himself, wept with exultation and relief. Oliver would never cease to amaze him. How had his introverted brother managed to talk someone into turning himself in to the police rather than take a ten-million-dollar payout?

"I need to get to Chicago as quickly as possible. Denise, can you please do me a favor? Call home and have Gibson pack a bag for me." His mind raced with everything he needed to do in order to get to Oliver. "I'll pick it up on the way to the airport. I'll call Captain Montez and arrange a flight. No, never mind, I don't need a bag. We're not staying overnight. I'll pack a bag for Oliver though."

Disregarding all the other people in the room, Denise walked over to her husband and embraced him, then kissed him tenderly. "It's okay. Slow down. He'll be home soon. Let's call Sarah and give her the good news. Then we'll call and arrange the flight. I'll pack you a bag, just in case. We'll all be waiting here for you."

Agent Greene spoke up, "I'll call and arrange your flight. I can pull some strings and get it done faster. If we take one of our planes it will be better than your own."

"Yes. Thanks. That sounds great." Simon could barely believe it was over. "There are people to call."

Deborah and Asher had come in to the library at some point during the commotion. "I'll make the rest of the calls, Simon. You go bring our Oliver home to us." Deborah hugged him.

It was Asher who made everyone stop the busyness. "Let's pray, then let's get to everything else, folks." Even the FBI agents seemed to agree with him. They formed a large circle and took hands. "Lord! Thank you for bringing Oliver to safety. Thank you for whatever it was you did to help him talk that man into turning himself in. Thank you for the miracles you worked. Amen."

Loud amens followed and the group dispersed back to the work at hand.

37

Simon walked as quietly as possible into the hospital room so that he would not wake Oliver. His brother's face was covered with bruises in assorted shades of purple, blue, green, and yellow, and there was an IV hydrating him. Had he really been gone for less than two weeks? He had lost weight during his ordeal, making him appear small and fragile. Yet Simon didn't see him as fragile or small. This man had not merely survived a terrible hardship; he had triumphed over it. Hearing from the doctor how very seriously battered Oliver was, and seeing so many of the injuries for himself, made him understand that his brother was stronger than most people knew, including Oliver himself.

Sitting down in the bedside chair, Simon searched his bag for his phone and speaker. He found them and put the classical music Oliver so loved on low volume. Oliver needed to rest, so Simon didn't want to wake him, but also couldn't bear leaving him. He pulled out his Bible and read while he listened to his brother's steady breathing and the soothing music of Vivaldi.

After perhaps twenty minutes, a stout dark-haired man entered the room. He apparently didn't care about waking Oliver from his much-needed rest, because his booming voice startled Simon and woke Oliver. "Good afternoon!" He held his hand out to Simon. "I'm Dr. Caspian." The doctor turned his attention to Oliver. "Are you ready to go home, sir? How are you feeling?"

Oliver blinked awake, noted Simon's presence with a nod, and said, "I'm pretty well. I think. I'm tired and I am more than ready to go home."

"Is he okay to go home?" Simon inquired. He had heard from another doctor, one named Wilcox, about Oliver's many injuries, and he didn't think it wise to rush to a discharge, though he wanted to bring his brother home.

The doctor looked questioningly at

Oliver, who saw the look and interceded. "This is my brother, Simon, and it is fine to speak in front of him."

"Nice to meet you," said the doctor with a quick glance at Simon. "You are badly bruised, so you need to make sure you take it easy for a couple of days and get plenty of fluids. There should be no more traces of dilaudid in your system. You are as healthy as you can be after going through what you did. I suggest following up with your primary at home. If you feel up to it, I can release you now, or if you would like you can stay one more night and go in the morning."

"I'll go home now. Thank you, Dr. Caspian."

Simon was relieved to hear his brother was okay, but wondered if it might be better for Oliver to stay one more night. He was about to voice his opinion, but in the end thought better of it. Oliver needed to be in charge after spending so much time as a prisoner.

"Well, it will be another hour or so. The nurse will come in to disconnect the IV and give you final instructions. Be well. Good luck, son." He patted Oliver on the shoulder and was gone.

Simon wasted no time once the doctor

was out of the room. He rushed to his brother and hugged him, carefully, afraid to hurt him. "Thank God you're safe! We've all been so worried for you."

Oliver pulled Simon closer to him and hugged tightly. "I'm so sorry. I shouldn't have let this happen."

"You didn't let this happen! It was done to you."

"If I had been more aware, or maybe known something, I should have known. It might not have happened. If I could have remembered the phone number or been able to speak to the people in the hospital the first time, it wouldn't have happened." Oliver dropped his eyes. "Mother would still be alive if I could have done something as simple as make a phone call."

Simon's heart broke for Oliver. "No. Mother was ill; she was hiding a condition from us and she died from the condition, not because you were missing. Being kidnapped was not your fault."

"I miss her. I'm not sure how I'll go on without her."

"I agree completely. But she taught us well, and I know we will go on." Simon looked over at his brother, and the two sat silently for several minutes. Then Simon decided it was time to get moving. "I brought you some clothes." He reached into the overnight bag and pulled out brown slacks and a tan sweater.

"Thanks, little brother. Maybe we should wait until the nurse disconnects this IV."

Simon laughed. "You were always the better thinker."

Oliver smiled as well too. "Remember when you tried to talk her into making me take you out on my date with Leslie Donovan? That was some pretty good thinking on your part. You almost talked her into it. You always did have her wrapped around your little finger."

"No one had her wrapped around any finger," said Simon. "Catherine Copeland never did anything she did not want to do."

They spoke about growing up with Catherine, and what an amazing woman and mother she had been. The longer they talked, the more Simon found that dwelling on the good memories helped make the pain fade away.

38

The crisp autumn air chilled Oliver to the bone. His suits were immaculately tailored, but he had lost so much weight over the past couple of weeks that he could feel this one hanging loosely on his gaunt frame. A crowd of mourners stood around the family, who sat in white wooden folding chairs near the white and gold coffin that held Catherine's remains. Sarah sat close to Oliver, sobbing into his chest. Simon sat on his other side, his eyes glistening with tears. Oliver's face was wet from unrestrained weeping. He listened to Allen Kennedy's words about eternal life, and said goodbye to his mother.

After the pastor finished speaking, the family each placed a red rose from Catherine's garden onto the coffin and returned to their seats. The legion of mourners began walking by the coffin, stopping to offer condolences. Oliver guessed there were hundreds of people at the funeral, and felt as if he should try and note each friend who had come to pay their respects, but the task was quite beyond him. He wasn't sure he was up to acknowledging each of them, much less trying to remember who every person was and what they had to say. However, the fact was that they mourned her too, and they sought some comfort in the comfort they offered. Oliver did his best to greet all of them individually. Sarah was by his side, accepting the sympathies with grace even through her tears. His beautiful daughter deftly provided the names Oliver needed as he returned the offered commiserations.

When the last of the guests had left, Oliver and the family stood and walked quietly to the parking lot. Long black cars waited to take them back to Cumberland, where there would be a reception for close friends and family. Oliver was worn and depleted. Sarah leaned into him, quiet now; perhaps she had emptied herself of tears as well. Deborah and Asher were quiet as well. Eileen alone talked for a few minutes. Deborah reached her mother's hand and squeezed it. Eileen stopped her monologue. Oliver relished the peace he would have for the ten-minute ride to the house before having to face the noise of the reception. He wished he could miss the gathering and just sit with his music, or better yet have silence for a little while. No one would blame him for going upstairs to his room. He had, after all, only just returned from a harrowing ordeal the day before yesterday. Denise might even order him to bed if he voiced his fatigue.

The idea was appealing. But he could hear Catherine's voice telling him that he was a Copeland, and Copelands were not selfish. He could offer his kindness and his presence to the many people who would be at the house out of kindness for him. He could hear his mother exhorting him not to be shy, and to try and be as convivial as his little brother. Her friends deserved it, and she deserved it. By the time the cars pulled into the drive, Oliver was prepared to face the reception.

Simon and Denise had exited the lead car and waited for Oliver, Sarah, and the Levines. As if Denise had been reading his mind, she headed for Oliver, took his hands and looked into his eyes. "You need to rest. I think you ought to go upstairs and leave the socializing to the rest of us."

He smiled, "No. Mother would want me to remain with all of you right now. I'll go upstairs in an hour."

"You're certain?" She squeezed his hands tighter.

"Yes, I'm certain. I promise if I become too tired or feel ill, I will retire immediately." He squeezed her hands in return, then straightened his back and led his family into Cumberland Manor.

There were many more people than Oliver had expected, most of them eating finger foods and chatting. It looked no different than any other party. He thought perhaps the mood would be muted, but he had to admit that Catherine would have wanted joy and laughter, even at her funeral. She never would have wanted people moping around on her account.

As Oliver walked past each little group of people, he could hear them speaking about Catherine. Many stopped their conversations to offer the family more condolences. Oliver felt exhausted, drained of energy and tears. He wished he had given in and simply walked upstairs to sleep, but he was doing as his mother would have wished. It wasn't the first time in his life that he had done what decorum demanded, and he knew it wouldn't be the last. He turned and took Phyllis Sumner's offered hand, trying to listen to her words.

"I will miss Catherine so very much, dear," she was telling him. "If there is anything I can do for you or Sarah, please let me know. In fact, I would love to spend some afternoons with Sarah and take her out for some girl time, perhaps be a mentor for her."

Sarah, who had not left Oliver's side, squeezed his other hand painfully, yet said, "Thank you, Mrs. Sumner. You are kind to offer."

Phyllis opened her mouth to speak again, but Simon had materialized. "Oliver, we need you in the sitting room." He turned his charming smile to his mother's friend. "Mrs. Sumner, thank you for coming today."

Oliver and Sarah entered the sitting room. The chair meant for Oliver beckoned him to it, and he gladly answered its call. He closed his eyes for a moment, letting it take his weight and give him the opportunity to rest. He sent up a prayer without words; he need the resolve to get through this, and he needed some energy. However, he was also deeply grateful for his family, and even the throng of friends who tried to allay the burden of grief the Copelands felt. Sarah's voice made his eyes snap open.

"Oh, Mrs. Treadway, thank you for coming. And thank you for the lovely flowers. Grandmother would have thought they were beautiful."

Lucy Treadway stood before him. Even through his exhaustion, Oliver couldn't help noticing how stunning she looked in a simple black skirt and jacket with low heels. Oliver could not think of anything to say to her. No words, no automatic greeting presented itself. He remained as he was and admired her exquisite grace.

"Daddy, Lucy Treadway came to the reception. Isn't that kind of her?" Once again Sarah squeezed his hand.

"Yes. Yes. Thank you, Lucy." He pulled his hand away from Sarah and offered it to the enchanting woman.

"Oliver, I am so relieved you're home. We held a prayer vigil at church. I was so worried for you. It must have been terrible. I don't want to ask you to talk about it, but when you're ready, I'm very willing to listen."

"Thank you," Oliver managed as he watched her walk away.

39

Deborah set the newspaper down and looked at Oliver with astonished pride. The front page of the *Belle Cay Star* carried a story from Chicago about the kidnapping and rescues, including an interview with Jimmy Ferguson. When the reporter had called Oliver's house for comment, he had chosen to comment only that he was happy to be home. Deborah was beaming. "Is this true? Why didn't you tell us what a hero you are? This Ferguson man says it was what you said to him and your kindness that convinced him to turn himself in. Oliver, you are so brave!"

Asher took the paper from his wife and read the article.

"I only did what anyone would have done.

I showed him a little kindness. I don't think many people have been nice to him in his life." Oliver hugged Sarah tighter as she snuggled next to him. "Some people have no idea of their worth."

"Big brother, I wonder whether you know your own worth, whether you know how remarkable you are."

Oliver blushed at the compliments and wished the newspaper had not chosen to run the story. His family's love warmed him as much as the crackling fire of the sitting room did. It had not been him but God who had worked miracles and brought him home to his family.

Joy and sadness intermingled in the room. Catherine was sorely missed as much as Oliver was celebrated. The entire family embraced one another a bit tighter.

"Are you tired, Oliver? There's another hour before lunch is served. Maybe you should go rest upstairs." Denise expertly checked her brother-in-law over with a light touch here and a skillful scrutinizing look there.

"Daddy, you do look tired," Sarah said, sounding like a concerned mother. "Go take a nap and I'll bring lunch up to you when it's ready."

Asha, who was curled up in Oliver's lap, pressed herself tighter against him as if she could hold him there by her will.

"My Unca Oliver doesn't need a nap, and neither do I," Misha answered for him.

"I will tell you when you need a nap, Little Man." said Denise. "Oliver, you will be honest if you feel ill or tired, won't you?"

"Yes, I will. I am resting here and now with all of you. But maybe you could let Henri know I only want soup for lunch, no bologna sandwich."

Simon cringed. "Yuck! No, you never have to eat bologna again. I promise."

"If I have anything to say about the matter, I will not eat it again. I don't even think I'll want a sandwich for a while."

Asher passed the newspaper on to Denise. "Oliver, Jimmy said you saved him as much as you saved yourself. He said you turned his life around and led him to Jesus. I don't think just any other person would have done that. It takes someone extraordinary and courageous."

"Can we stop talking about how courageous I am and start just enjoying my being here?"

Asha sat up in Oliver's lap and took his face into her little hands. "Don't ever go away again, Honey. I missed you."

"I missed you too. I missed all of you."

Part Two

1

The florescent lights of the interrogation room flickered and buzzed. They did nothing for Oliver's headache, nor did the uncomfortable chair help him feel any better. The FBI had moved out of Cumberland and into the Belle Cay police station. Most of the agents had gone, but a few remained to continue the investigation into the kidnapping. Agent Greene had been interviewing Oliver for what felt like hours.

"Oliver, there was no convention in Chicago. Are you sure that's why you were there?"

"I went because Nathan Westley wanted me to go to the convention and talk to other investors. He wants me to…invest in this app he's developing. I checked everything else so carefully, it never occurred to me to check if there was… actually a convention." He was tired and his words were coming a bit more slowly than he wanted them to come. "Why would he lie about something like that?"

As the interview had continued, it became clear that Nathan had lied about many things. Oliver had recounted the events at the club that evening and afterwards countless times. Each time, he understood a little more that Westley had been a con man, and that Oliver, the dupe, had eagerly fallen for every part of it.

Agent Artois spoke up, "Frank O'Neil has implicated this Nathan Westley and given us another name for him. Steve Fischer. Is that name familiar to you?"

"No, I only knew him as Nathan Westley. Jimmy referred to a W from time to time. It never occurred to me…" Oliver's heart sank. The man who he had thought of as a friend was the man behind his near death. Oliver was not a friend or mentor to Nathan, only a ripe bank account ready to be plucked.

"We don't think Steve Fischer is any more his name than Nathan Westley is, but perhaps that name can help us find other victims. We need more evidence to really make an airtight case against him. In fact, we'd like you to help us. We believe with your assistance we could bring down enough charges to imprison him for life." Artois's black eyes were as intense as his words.

Oliver was frozen with fear. How could he possibly help bring a criminal in? He was not strong enough nor smart enough. He couldn't do it. Though he wanted to, he couldn't even open his mouth to protest. He breathed in and prayed; he breathed out and prayed. His mouth finally opened. "What is it that I could possibly do?"

Greene was almost exuberant as he answered. "Westley doesn't know that you know he was behind this. He knows that he was described as a "person of interest," but he gave his interview to the police and he has not been formally described as a suspect. As far as we can tell, he thinks he's in the clear. More than that, he's probably desperate to get some sort of payout, since he didn't get any money from your 'investment' or from his attempted kidnapping."

Artois leaned forward. "He also doesn't know Frank has turned on him. And remember, he thinks he has you hook, line, and sinker. He believes you're..." Artois seemed to rethink whatever he was about to say. "He underestimates your mental sharpness," the agent continued tactfully. "He probably believes you still trust him. As a result, we believe Westley will try and finish the con if he thinks there's a chance."

"You want me to con the con man?" Oliver considered it. Could he do that? "I'm not sure that I'm capable of that sort of deception. My memory doesn't like to play along."

Artois' enthusiasm for his plan would not be deflated. "You would continue to meet with him, just as you have. You'd wear a wire, and even an earpiece if that makes you feel better. You would never be alone. Our people would always be nearby."

With his stomach sour from nerves and his head swimming with fear, Oliver breathed a prayer. "Okay, I'll do it."

Agent Artois nearly leapt at the agreement. "Great! Make a call and schedule a meeting with him. We'll take it from there."

2

Langley Barnett entered Oliver's office exactly on time for their meeting. The large ex-Marine smiled broadly and grasped Oliver's hand. "Welcome back! Oliv...that is, Mr. Copeland, let me be the first to welcome you back to work. I heard some of what you experienced, and I have to say you, sir, are a hero!"

Oliver was at a loss for a response. He looked to Marcus who quickly shut his agape mouth. The sight of his normally collected assistant in a state of surprise brought a smile to Oliver's face. "Thank you, Langley. Please, have a seat. It is good to be home. I don't know if I deserve the title of hero, though. Let's save that term for veterans like you, and the police officers and other first responders that played a role in my freedom."

Barnett's impossibly large frame folded itself onto the office chair. "I heard you played a large role in your freedom and the capture of the men responsible."

"Actually, Langley, that is one of the reasons I asked to see you. There is one more man who needs to be caught, and I need your financial expertise. The FBI wants us to set up an account through the company, which can be used to make this man think he is receiving money from us. When I transfer funds from that account to his account, the FBI will trace it, and they'll be able to temporarily freeze the account so the money doesn't actually go anywhere. I will personally insure the funds, so there won't be any risk to the company."

Langley looked excited to be part of the intriguing mission. "Ah, yes! I can do that. It's a simple matter. This is to be in your name, I assume? I'll have it ready for you by this afternoon. I can even make it appear as if it has been used for years." He took out a notebook and scribbled notes to himself.

"Thank you so much, Langley. I knew I could count on you. Please let me know as soon as it's ready. Now, if you'll excuse me, I have much work to catch up on." Oliver stood and offered his hand to the CFO. He watched in silent wonder as the man shook his hand and left the office with almost a skip in his step. Up to now, Langley had resented him, and had taken every opportunity possible to demean him.

It was true that there was a great deal of work to do, but Oliver wanted to get this Nathan Westley situation behind him. He dialed Westley's number even as he doubted he would get an answer. To his surprise there was an answer.

"Hello. This is Nathan Westley."

"Nathan, it's Oliver Copeland. I was calling to make sure you are okay."

There was a momentary silence, followed by an excited shout. "Oliver! I am so happy to hear your voice! I was giving you time to grieve your mother, and I had heard you were kidnapped or something. That had to be tabloid fiction. Is it true?"

"Believe it or not, it is true. I was mugged when I left that club we went to. I couldn't find you anywhere, and I was kidnapped. We got them all, though, and I am safe back home. I was worried that something may have happened to you as well." The lies tasted sour in Oliver's mouth, but he reminded himself that he needed to make the con artist comfortable. He was furious at the way Nathan or Steven or whatever his name was had treated him. The idea of retribution made lying a little easier, and even that made him angry. Years of suppressing his emotions worked to Oliver's benefit, and he kept his voice pleasant. "I hope you're alright."

"I can't believe it1! I feel awful. I thought you had left with a woman and had decided to ditch the convention. I was so involved in meetings and presentations that it didn't even occur to me you were anything but fine. I am so sorry!"

"Well, I'm fine now, and back into the swing of things at last. I'm ready to get back to business, and I want to meet with you regarding in that app. I want to hear what all the people at the convention thought about it." Oliver waited quietly, like a fisherman waiting for the fish to take the bait. He did not have to wait long.

"I could certainly use the investment. There are things I need to do with the app and I am at a stand-still."

"Well, I am looking forward to making some money. Nathan, let's meet at the club tomorrow for lunch, say one o'clock." Oliver looked at Marcus as he spoke, and Marcus recorded the appointment.

The rest of the day went quickly as Oliver caught up with business. Each meeting included extended sympathies for his loss or astonished exclamations at his surviving a kidnapping, and many of them contained both. Oliver had never been one to appreciate a pat answer, but he had fallen to using them now. How many times had he repeated, "Thank you so much; Catherine will be deeply missed," or "I am blessed to be alive and well"? Neither statement could carry the profundity of experience or emotion. No one outside the family's inner circle knew even part of what Oliver had suffered. He did not expect them to understand it. To them it was like a thrilling novel or exciting movie, but even in hindsight Oliver could not make light of it. When he thought about the whole experience, he would remind himself that his captivity had taught him to be free of the shame and pride that had bound him for so many years. The spiritual chains that imprisoned him had been loosed, and freedom was his to enjoy. He was still furious, though, that someone had thrown his kindness in his face and treated him as if he were stupid. The fact that Oliver had nearly been killed hung in his mind and heart, at times triggering anger, and other times producing joy and relief, or an obligation to live the rest of his life well.

Memories of physical chains, locked doors, violence, and drugs lurked in the back of his mind, trying to resurface. His ire fueled their power even now. In his heart, the Holy Spirit reminded him that He had set him free, and even while he had been locked away, he had the only freedom that mattered. If he had not been kidnapped, would he ever have known the liberty of no longer hiding his impairments? Would he appreciate the deluge of blessings his life was, the food and the house and the possessions that God had given him, a level of comfort and opulence that most people could only dream of? Would Jimmy have been able to recognize his need for Jesus? The nightmare of his captivity was over, but until he had brought justice to Nathan, Oliver didn't think he would be free.

3

The tiny device fixed into Oliver's tie pin didn't weigh much, but it felt heavy anyway. Though Agents Green and Artois had told Oliver not to try and get Westley to say anything, and that he should let the conversation flow naturally, he worried that he might misstep and ruin the operation. Agent Artois had explained that this would be only the first of several meetings, and with each one they would gather more evidence. After testing the microphone and assuring Oliver that people would be listening and close enough to act if needed, Agent Artois sent Oliver off to the club to meet the grifter who was now the mark.

Oliver watched Nathan approach the

table and stood to greet him. "Thank you for meeting me," Oliver said. "I'm happy to see you again. How have things been?" Oliver envisioned every word he spoke exiting his mouth and written on a legal pad.

"I've been well. So sorry about everything you've been through. It must have been horrible!" Nathan sat and waved the waitress over in one fluid motion.

"I'm blessed to be alive and well," answered Oliver as he swallowed his rage. "Have you gotten things worked out financially? You aren't staying at the rental any longer."

"Well, I managed a personal loan from a friend of my father. I'm living at the house during renovations and squeaking by." Nathan perused the menu as he spoke. "I'm grateful this is a business expense for you. I've been living off bachelor rations. I didn't eat this poorly even in college."

Oliver recognized the request for another loan. He had blank checks from the special account Langley Barnett had created, as well as a cashier's check for the two-million-dollar bogus investment. Oliver was keenly aware that he couldn't offer the vile man any money, so he waited for a request. "I'm sorry to hear that. What are you eating – baloney and cheese sandwiches? That can't be much fun."

Nathan laughed. "It's not all that bad. But I could use a little money until this gets straightened out. Could you extend me another loan? Perhaps ten thousand?"

Oliver faked joviality. "That will buy you some nice groceries. I guess you need to pay some staff too. Sure. It's no problem." He pulled out the checkbook, flipped it open, and readied his pen. "When do you think you might be getting this back to me? I'm not sure how confident I am in investing in someone who has borrowed such a great deal of money." He watched Nathan squirm and hoped he had not overplayed his hand.

"The bank has assured me that it will all be squared within the month. You know I'm good for it. I just don't want to upset my father by letting his friend think I'm in trouble."

Oliver wrote the check that Nathan had requested, and as they continued the conversation, he wondered how he could never noticed the man's pomposity before now. How had he missed the many incongruities that he saw now? Yes, his suit was expensive, but it was one of only two he ever wore. That Nathan had made a small investment in appearing to be a wealthy young business man was obvious now. Oliver bristled at the realization that, upon closer inspection, Nathan, or whoever he was, was very clearly not what he seemed.

"…ready to get moving with developing this app, are you ready to make some money?" Nathan said with excitement.

Oliver returned to the present. "Tell me what I am going to get for my money." Each claim he got out of Nathan would be used against him later.

"I am prepared to give you 30% of the returns. Market research suggests we can sell the app for $8.99, and after the first four months, we'll be pulling in pure profit of about $500K a month, which should only increase over time. I think that if we put your name on the app, we'll have an even greater income. The Copeland name has credibility, and it is due to you that I'll be able to do this. I would like to honor you by calling it the Copeland Mobile Administrator. The CMA is going to ensure that your great-great-grandchildren will be wealthy."

Oliver had no concerns that his descendants would ever have to worry about money, but he had to let Nathan believe that he was falling for it. "I'm looking forward to it, Nathan. I have the check ready for you.

Two million dollars. It is a cashier's check, so please be careful. Do you have the contract?"

Nathan extracted a contract from his pristine briefcase and pushed it across the table to Oliver. "Here it is, just as we discussed." He appeared scarcely able to contain himself. "Sign that, we'll get you a copy, and we're set." Nathan's hand remained open and reaching, eager for the money.

Oliver knew the moment he gave him the check, he would not see Nathan again. He needed some more meetings with him to implicate him in the abduction. "Listen, I have some ideas. I have the money; you have the know-how. I'd love to make even more money by extending this partnership and creating some more business and social apps."

Nathan sat forward. "Really? Wow, yeah, we could do that."

Oliver took a bite of his king salmon and realized he had switched places with Nathan. Nathan was the big fish on the hook now, and Oliver was the one doing the con.

4

Oliver's footsteps echoed in the vacant halls of Cumberland. Servants bustled about, keeping the house running and immaculate as the lonely lord of the manor walked from room to room. How could the absence of one person empty a home and make it merely a house? "Lord, will this ever feel like home again without her?" Oliver prayed aloud, knowing that only God would hear him. The sound of his ringing phone disturbed the quiet, startling him. He laughed at himself for jumping at the sound. How long had it been since he had laughed at anything, especially himself? His phone's screen told him the caller was Lucy Treadway. He wondered why she was calling, but couldn't help notice that the sight of her name made him happy. The phone rang for the third time before Oliver remembered that he was supposed to answer. "Hello."

"Oliver, how are you?"

Oliver paused for a beat to see if she was going to continue or if she genuinely wanted an answer to the question. He was pleased to see that her interest was sincere. "I'm well, thank you. How are you?"

"I'm fine. Thanks so much for asking. Are you sure you're okay? You've been through so much."

"I suppose you could say I am well considering the circumstances. My health is good. I've gotten back to working out again. I'm concerned about Sarah, though; she won't go out with her friends anymore. She stays by my side when she's home and she calls me between classes when she's at school. I..." He weighed how much he could tell his friend. "I'm having some nightmares about being held hostage. I keep thinking I'm in that horrible place. I can't get warm enough at night. I've got a blanket and a down comforter on the bed and I continue to shiver."

"Oliver, I'm sorry," Lucy said, and Oliver could tell from her tone that she really meant it. "I know such a harrowing experience doesn't just go away. If you want to talk about it, I am always here for you."

"Thank you." He knew it was true, and the relief he felt caught him by surprise. His burden was lighter as he understood he could share it with Lucy.

"I know this is a lot to ask," Lucy said, "but I was hoping that you could help me chaperone Maya's Sweet Sixteen. I think the entire junior class will be there. So many teenagers all trying to outdo one another with how grown-up they are. Sarah will be there, of course, and I thought maybe you could accompany me. You don't really have to chaperone. Honestly, that was just a flimsy excuse for me to ask you to come. I do hope you'll come. I would love to have you there. I think I need to have you there." She seemed to realize she was rambling, and suddenly stopped with an exhalation of breath.

Oliver sorted through it all silently, and she did not push him to answer her immediately. She was asking him on a date. Fear tried to seize his heart. He wasn't sure he could trust anyone. Kelly had hurt him. Nathan had swindled him. Would Lucy be any different?

She was different, though. During the

years he had known her, she had always been kindhearted, genuine, and compassionate. He broke fear's grip on him and answered her. "Yes, I would love to. Will you do me a favor and text me the details? My memory isn't very good, and I absolutely do not want to forget this."

Lucy's laugh carried the unmistakable sound of relief. "Thank you, Oliver. Thank you."

Emboldened by courage, Oliver added, "The Harvest Festival is this Saturday. Would you do me the honor of accompanying me? Of course, your children are invited as well." Butterflies flew furiously in his stomach as he waited for her response.

There was no pause. "I would love to. Maya and Edwin were already planning to attend. We go every year, in fact. It will be really special to be your guests. Thank you."

The two talked for another hour until Lucy sadly proclaimed her phone battery was about to die.

5

Cathy was light in Simon's arms, probably because she clung so tightly to him on the invigoratingly cold afternoon of the Harvest Festival. He felt deeply happy walking among the game booths toward the bounce house. Denise was by his side holding Misha's hand. Kyle and Jackson walked a few feet ahead of their parents, trying to act as independently as possible while they kept up a constant stream of chatter with Sarah, Maya, and Edwin.

"Honey, look at that bear! Will you win it for me?" Asha pulled Oliver with all her tiny might toward a game table decorated with giant stuffed animals.

"Asha, that bear is bigger than you are. You don't need another toy," Asher interjected, probably knowing he would be the one who had to carry the massive doll around for the remainder of the day.

"She might not need the bear, but she wants it so much. Please let me try." Oliver could not say no to her, and so the entire family stopped at the game and the men bought tickets for their chance to blow up a balloon with a water pistol.

Simon tried to set Cathy down so he could join Oliver and Asher in the game, but she wouldn't relinquish her tight embrace. "Sweetheart, I need to put you down, just for a minute."

Lucy stepped forward, "Let me take her while you play." She reached out her arms and Cathy joyfully went to her.

"Thank you," said Simon. He picked up his water gun and aimed for the small target.

The table volunteer, Brad Peterson, shouted, "On your mark, get set, go!" He pressed a button and music began as water shot out of the guns to hit the targets.

The family cheered their men on as they all watched the brightly colored balloons grow larger. Asha rooted on both Oliver and Ash. "Go, Honey! You can do it, daddy!"

Cathy, too, had decided she needed a gigantic bear, and rooted for Simon, "Daddy,

daddy blower it up, daddy!" she chanted. She glanced sideways and placed her little hand over Lucy's mouth. "Stop saying, 'Go Oliver,' I want daddy to win."

Lucy laughed, "Okay, I'll stop. May I have my mouth back, please?"

"Promise you'll say, 'Go daddy.'" The child said sternly.

"Very well. Go, daddy!"

Cathy moved her hand and resumed cheering for her father and the coveted prize.

The first race ended with Simon victoriously popping the balloon. The huge bear was handed over to Cathy, and the forlorn look on Asha's face spurred the men on to a second race. This time, Cathy not only allowed Lucy to root for Oliver, but joined in as well.

Oliver was triumphant in the second race and presented the trophy to Asha, who was clearly delighted. "My dear princess, your bear, as you requested."

"Thank you, Honey!" She took the giant stuffed bear in her little arms and hugged it tightly to her chest. She and Cathy walked together, each pretending that the toys were not a burden. They talked back and forth about their new pets, giving them names and planning a tea party for them for the next day.

Two hours later, after the bounce house, homemade ice cream, and arts and crafts booth, and with the mammoth stuffed animals displacing Daniel from his stroller, the family came upon a new exhibit to the annual festival. Lucy Treadway's family had long supported animal rights campaigns, so she had arranged for a small animal-free circus as well as an information table from Born Free America to come to the festival.

"The addition of the circus to the festival has boosted donations. Early estimates say that so far we have taken in nearly one and half times what we took in last year. The children's charities are going to have a very good year. Thank you, Lucy, for suggesting and organizing this," Simon said. He had been impressed with Lucy, and had hoped for some time that Oliver would give her a chance. Now she was proving herself to be a great fit with him and the family.

He knew Oliver was still reserved, and that most of his brother's attention was geared toward apprehending Nathan Westley. He wanted to encourage Oliver in any way he could to further his companionship with Lucy. "Mother would have been so grateful. I think she would have loved the idea of promoting a deserving organization while supporting the children's charities." He looked to his brother for a response, but got none from the pensive man. "Don't you think so, Oliver? Wouldn't Mother be impressed?"

"Mother was not an easy woman to impress," Oliver said, and then paused. Simon's stomach dropped like a roller-coaster car on a steep hill. "But yes, I believe she would have thought this extraordinary." He took Lucy's hand. "You are extraordinary."

Simon's heart leapt at the sight of Oliver letting someone beyond his carefully constructed wall. But Misha quickly pulled his attention as he tugged his father's hand.

"Daddy," said the son who so reminded him of Oliver, as he pointed out a photo of an elephant wearing an iron shackle on its thick leg. "Why is that ephalant... I mean el-a-phant, why is he wearing that bracelet?"

"May I answer?" Lucy asked. She bent down to Misha's level, and all the children gathered around her, even Sarah, Maya, and Edwin. "Some people take baby elephants away from their mommies and homes in Africa and Asia and put them in circuses or zoos. Circuses chain them up with a manacle, which is that bracelet and chain, to a spike in the ground. The little elephant tries to walk away, but it can't because it hurts too much and he isn't strong enough."

"Oh, no!" cried Cathy. "That's so mean!"

"Yes, it is mean," Lucy continued. "Eventually the elephant stops trying to get away. The people who are keeping him know he's grown big and strong enough to pull the spike out of the ground. But the elephant doesn't know how strong he is. That bracelet keeps him thinking he's chained up, and he does whatever the circus people tell him to do, even though he might be very sad."

Misha was crying. "Poor baby. I don't want to see the circus, daddy. I can't let them think it's okay to be so mean. I'm gonna tell those people. Where are they?"

Kyle, his face red with anger, stood with his brother. "Let's tell 'em!"

Simon nodded in agreement. "We will write letters to send to the circuses that keep animals like that tonight when we get home. However, this circus doesn't have any animals. It has acrobats, clowns, and people who can do some incredible things. We can see this show, and it will tell the other ones that they don't have to have animals doing tricks to amaze us."

"I think we have lots of letters to write. We should call them or go tell them in person," Jackson said, probably trying to get out of the work of writing.

"Maybe we can call some of them, but we'll still write, son." Simon squeezed Jackson's shoulder. His young son already considered hugging too immature.

6

"That man is going to pay for what he put me through!" Oliver was pacing back and forth in the library where he and Lucy were supposed to be enjoying a post-dinner conversation. "He called me this afternoon, and in a few days he's coming here to finalize terms. He still thinks he's getting five million dollars out of me. He's getting a pair of handcuffs and a trip to prison! He'll regret messing with me."

Lucy fidgeted in her seat. "Can we please talk about something other than Nathan Westley? We've been seeing each other for nearly two weeks, and every conversation ends with you explaining all over again how angry you are at him and how you're doing everything in your power to get back at him. I know you want justice, but it seems like you're talking about a lot more than justice."

Oliver gaped at her. How could she speak that way? Was this the moment when she finally showed her true colors, when she revealed an icy self-absorbed cruel heart? Oliver had made himself believe that Lucy was not like Kelly. Maybe he had been very, very wrong. "I'm sorry, but I want my vengeance, and I think I'm entitled to it. That man stole my dignity, abducted me, imprisoned me, and for all intents and purposes tortured me. I'm sorry if that happens to be on my mind and if I need to talk about it sometimes!"

"That's just the thing. You're not talking about the abduction and what it did to you. All you're talking about is how you can't wait to get back at Nathan, to make him personally pay, to ruin him." Lucy walked into Oliver's path and made him cease his pacing. "You're not free. You said you're free and you claim to be liberated from the fears and shame that you said held you prisoner. But you're still a prisoner; you're still chained down by your desire for retribution. Nathan Westley owns your body and your mind now even more than he did when you were in that house, because you can't stop thinking about how much you want to make him suffer. You can't realize that you're the one who's suffering. You're like the circus elephants who could be free but don't know their own strength. You're wearing chains of pride and bitterness."

Oliver's anger burned his mind and spit fire from his mouth. "No! If there is anything trying to hold me, it's you! How dare you lecture me about my own feelings? How dare you presume to tell me what I am and am not allowed to feel? I will not be manipulated!" He was breathing hard, his chest heaving with the effort to hurt her as her words had hurt him. "I want this man caught! I can do something about it. Me! I'm not the helpless…" He searched for the word he wanted, could not find it and chose another. "cripple that you hope I'll be. I am the only one who can help the FBI catch him. If you don't want to help me, then get out!" He tried to walk past her, but she stepped in his way. He turned his back instead. She touched his arm and he withdrew it.

She reached out again, took his hand and walked to face him. "I could never think that about you. You're confusing me with someone else. You are not behaving like the man I've come to love."

Her words stunned Oliver and doused the fury-fueled fire that had swept through him. Oliver kept his hand in hers and walked to the settee with her. He was silent as he processed her words and his, breath prayers and peace grew over the ashes of his pride. She didn't interrupt his contemplation. After a few minutes, he said, "Okay. I'm here and I am truly sorry. Let me try and rearrange the 'I's and the 'you's. Tell me what you mean about me not being free. How could I not be free?" Her words resonated within him. Hadn't he already told himself the same thing?

Lucy exhaled a long and slow breath as her shoulders relaxed and her eyes brightened. "Let me ask you a question. Don't you trust God? You're lying to this man to get revenge. You're delighted by the thought of revenge. I thought God said vengeance was His. If you trust Him, you'll stop lying and let God take care of this."

"Don't I have to lie to catch him? I'm just doing what the FBI tells me to do."

"The FBI doesn't answer to God. You do. The truth will set you free, Oliver. Lies destroy. Love doesn't lie. You are better and stronger than that. You have Jesus, you have the Holy Spirit within you. The FBI doesn't know His power."

"The Truth will set me free." He shook his head. "I thought it had. It appears there is more to be freed from. What if he gets away? What if the FBI never can catch him for this?"

Lucy smiled. "What if he does?"

"There's nothing wrong with lying in order to keep other people from being hurt," Oliver declared. "Do you remember the Bible story of Rahab the prostitute? She hid two Israelite spies and lied when she was asked if she knew where they were. The Bible says that she was a hero. She is mentioned by name in Hebrews 11, the chapter that talks about people with great faith."

"She wasn't a hero of the faith because she lied," Lucy observed. "She was a hero of the faith because she trusted God even when it was difficult. What do you think that means for you?"

"Well..." He considered the possibilities. "I don't know. If I trust God, I suppose I have to trust Him with everything." He was silent for a while, praying, trying to listen for God's voice. At last he looked at Lucy. "I can give this to God."

She set her head on his chest. "Are the 'I's and 'you's rearranged? I'll do the same. I will stop accusing and blaming and take some responsibility too. I need you."

The two remained like that until the quiet was broken by Sarah, Maya, and Edwin bursting into the room. "We're home!" Sarah proclaimed. "Daddy, how are you? What did you eat for dinner?"

"The movie was great!" said Edwin, ignoring Sarah's worried questions to her father. Suddenly he noticed the couple on the couch. "Maybe we should go back out and get some ice cream." He smiled and winked at the other two teens.

"No," said Oliver as he rose from the couch. "We have ice cream here. Let's enjoy some together. Sarah, you know that Lucy was responsible for my dinner. I ate, and I ate well."

Sarah took her father's hand. "Sorry, daddy. Thank you for making me go out. I trusted Lucy to take care of you, and I can see she did."

Lucy stood as well. "Edwin, Maya, go to the kitchen and we'll meet you there. Sarah, your dad takes as much care of me as I do of him, and probably more. Isn't he a good father? You should enjoy being sixteen, and let him take care of you." Lucy stroked Sarah's blonde hair.

"I'm sorry. I've always taken care of

Daddy, and I can't lose him. Everyone else is gone." Sarah was forlorn. She stood holding Oliver's hand, tears flowing down her cheeks.

"Honey," said Oliver. He took his hand out of hers and wrapped his daughter in his arms. "You have lost some important people in your life, but you haven't lost everyone. I love how we take care of each other, but sweetie, it's okay. I am stronger now, and I am going to do my best not to get hurt. But let's trust God to take care of us, okay?" He cradled her in his arms, rocking her like a baby.

Sarah sniffed and wiped the tears from her face. "I'll try, daddy."

7

The crowd cheered for the beautiful Maya Treadway, her curly brown hair arranged in a complex swirl atop her head, her sparkling pink dress spinning about her as she danced with her uncle in the place of the father who had died when she was a child. However, Oliver wasn't watching the birthday girl; he was watching her mother. Lucy glowed as she, like almost every other person in the room, watched Maya dance.

Lucy's black hair was styled simply and hung down her back. Her burgundy dress enhanced her inherent elegance. The lights of the rented hall shined on the jewels she wore. Oliver almost didn't want to stop watching her, but he did in order to invite her to the dance floor. He didn't enjoy dancing, especially in a situation which would draw attention. For her, though, he felt he could do it. "Will you do me the honor of dancing with me?"

"Yes" She took his hand let him lead her to the dance floor.

Oliver placed his arms around her waist and she stepped in closer to him. Somehow, the dancing didn't bother him the way he thought it would. For some reason he wasn't as self-conscious as he normally was. There were no lights, no band, and no spectators. The world was her in his arms, her head on his shoulder, and her scent making him drunk with bliss. He knew he loved her. She had told him she loved him, but was her love enough to accept his quirks and the many parts of himself that were less than she deserved? How would she feel when he forgot her birthday or couldn't share a fork or a cup with her? How would she feel when his whole self was revealed to her? The band had materialized during Oliver's musing, and Oliver was suddenly aware of every eye that watched his awkward dancing. The bright lights were giving him a headache. To his relief the song ended, and without consulting Lucy, Oliver walked off the dance floor to the relative safety of the table where they had eaten dinner.

"What's wrong?" Lucy asked, her concern showing in her voice and the crease of her brow.

"Did I say something was wrong? Nothing's the matter. The song was over, that's all."

She looked at him through slightly squinted eyes, as if trying to see through him. "Are you sure? Do you have a headache? Are you tired?"

Before he could stop himself, he snapped, "I said that nothing is the matter! I'm not a child." He wished he had agreed that he had a headache, as it would have given him an excuse to go home.

Lucy raised an eyebrow. "You'll have to forgive me. I was unaware that it was improper to show concern for you." She stood up. "I'm going to talk to Shane's brother Bill."

Oliver watched the widow go speak to her brother-in-law. He wanted to call out to her, but he didn't dare cause a scene. "I'm an idiot," he said quietly to no one in particular.

"No, daddy, but maybe you are acting like a child." Sarah said, materializing behind him as she and Edwin approached the table.

"Sir," said Edwin, "I would never accuse you of being childish. But I think you should go after my mother. I don't want her to lose you. Go to her, please."

Oliver got up and Sarah took hold of his arm, "If you let her break up with you, it will ruin Maya's Sweet Sixteen, and it will ruin you."

He smiled at his overdramatic daughter. "Don't worry." He navigated the crowd, ignoring the greetings from people he didn't recognize and a few he did before finding Lucy chatting with Bill and his wife Margaret. "Excuse me. Bill, how are you? Margaret, you look beautiful. Lucy, may I speak with you, please?"

"Bill, Margaret, it was so nice talking to you. I'll see you Thursday for dinner." She gave Oliver a stern look. "If you have something to say to me then we can go outside." She didn't wait for a response, but walked outside and let him follow her.

Happy to be away from the noise and glare of the party, he let out breath he hadn't known he was holding. "I'm so sorry. I started thinking, and it got to a point it shouldn't have. I am not good enough for you, Lucy, and I'm worried you'll figure that out."

"Oliver! Am I going to constantly have to

tell you what you should already know? You are an amazing, strong, intelligent man. I couldn't ask for a better man."

"Do you want an honest answer? Yes, you will probably have to tell me that constantly." He spread his hands. "You know that I have many, many issues from my accident, and if you say you love me, then you have to be okay with those things all the time. I am not sure you truly appreciate how..." He searched his mind for a better word, but none came to him. "How weird I am."

"Yes, I do. You're a clean freak. Guess what: so am I! You don't like to share a glass or eat off the same fork as someone else. Please! I can deal with that. You don't secretly put on a clown nose when no one is watching, do you? Or is it that you have a locked room filled with big-eyed dolls? I'm weird too."

Oliver was laughing at his own absurdity now. "No, you're perfect! Nothing about you could make me think otherwise."

"That is too much to live up to. I have quirks too, mister."

"Go ahead and shock me."

"Okay. Ugly feet disgust me. Yours are fine, but if you're with me you'll be required to get a pedicure once a month. I've been told I talk in my sleep. And I don't drink cow's milk, ever. But I can't get enough of other dairy products."

"You see? You are perfect!" Oliver took her hands in his. "I really am sorry. Sometimes I get so much in my own head. Please forgive me."

"I forgive you. Now come inside for thirty more minutes, then I'll let you go home to some quiet. Oh, and you're coming to dinner Thursday at Bill's place. Put it in your phone right now. Pick me up at 6:45."

Oliver took out his phone, putting the date in his calendar before walking back into the cacophony of Maya's party. Lucy really was almost perfect. What she had announced as flaws only made him love her more.

8

Oliver was sweating, even in the cold November afternoon. The wire he wore poked his chest and accused him of betraying his commitment to Agents Greene and Artois. He inhaled for a count of six, then stopped. He exhaled a prayer, braced himself, and said, "Nathan, have a seat." He pointed to the chair opposite his on the rose garden patio. "Thank you, Ian."

The butler watched Nathan sit down and left to get a tray of coffee and tea.

"I'm excited to get this partnership going, Oliver. I feel like we should have done things this way from the beginning. I couldn't ask to go into business with a finer man."

Oliver swallowed his disgust at the man's

smarminess. "Mr. Westley…" Even saying that name felt like a lie, he no longer wanted to tell. "No. I would love to call you by your real name. What is it?"

Nathan went pale and his mouth fell open. A moment later he recovered and gave what sounded like a real laugh. "You are funny! Nathan Westley is my name. I do have another name I went by in the past for some business dealings that involved MI6. You must have done some digging, as well you should, of course. But that is in the past, over and done with." Lies poured from his mouth the way lava flowed from an erupting volcano. Oliver said nothing; he only watched the man's face. "I'll have to share that story with you sometime. Of course, most of it is still classified." Oliver continued to wait. "I, well, I have had a few dealings with MI6 and the CIA. Perhaps one day when it is all declassified I should write a book. No one would ever believe it was a true story."

Finally Oliver spoke. "I'm sure you have some great stories." He turned to Ian who had arrived with the tray. "Thank you, Ian. I'll pour."

"Yes, sir." Someone who didn't know Ian very well would have missed the quick glare he shot at Nathan and seen only the smile and nod he gave Oliver.

Oliver poured Nathan a cup of coffee. "I have to tell you some difficult things." He then poured himself some tea and added cream and sugar. "I have lied to you. I know that you were behind my mugging and my kidnapping. I know that you are not Nathan Westley and that you think you conned me for two million dollars as well as the..." He paused to look at sheet of paper. "$228,750 in incidentals."

Nathan had turned to stone. His jaw was the only part of his alabaster face that moved as he clenched his teeth. He then opened his mouth to interrupt, but Oliver did not allow him.

"I know you thought you were going to get another five million out of me. It's not going to happen. I can't lie to you any longer. It isn't who I am." Oliver leaned forward on the table. "I am not the bitter and prideful man you tried to make me. You hurt me, not only physically but emotionally as well. I thought you were genuinely my friend. I let pride make me believe you, even when I shouldn't have. I was humiliated and beaten and held in conditions that I didn't think I could stomach. I was not by my mother's side when she died. I was not here for my daughter because of your avarice."

Nathan opened his mouth again, but no words emerged. He closed his mouth and opened it again, looking like a guppy. Oliver actually felt a little empathy; the man clearly wanted to say something to defend himself but didn't have the words. How could he? There was no defense.

"I wanted to get retribution for everything you took from me," Oliver continued. "I wanted you to experience the pain you caused me. I still want justice, but now I am trusting God for that justice. I have chosen to forgive you for the horrors you put me and my family through."

It seemed that finally the man across from him was able to find some words. "You don't need to forgive me! Find some forgiveness for yourself. You can't be conned if you aren't greedy yourself. You were desperate for someone to respect you, so I gave you that. You loved my fawning over you. You loved to imagine yourself as the big business man. You gave me all that money so you could be the big man, not because you're so benevolent."

"Maybe what you say is right. Maybe it's not. But would you have come back to steal another five million dollars if you weren't also greedy?" Oliver smiled at the man and hoped he would continue his tirade. He was not disappointed.

"Yeah, I'm greedy. I stole two and a quarter million dollars from you. And even when the ransom plans fell through because your family found you, I still thought I could get more. I've stolen from a lot of people, and I will steal from a lot more. There's nothing you can do to stop me. You're a damaged human being! What did you tell Jimmy, that you are cognitively impaired? That is an understatement. You're an imbecile! No one will believe you, and you couldn't manage to tell the police anyway. I made sure I am not connected with the lowlifes who work for me. I'm smarter than you, smarter than them, and smarter than pretty much anyone who would ever try to face me. Go ahead. Do your best. You won't see me again." Nathan stood up to leave, knocking his chair over as he turned away from Oliver.

"I wouldn't have called the police. I was already working with the FBI. You'll see me again when I face you in court and tell the judge what you did. Of course, you could just save yourself the misery, be a man, and confess."

By now several men and women led by

Greene and Artois were rushing toward Nathan or whatever he was really called. One of them, Oliver couldn't tell which, shouted, "Nathan Westley, down on your knees, hands open and over your head! Now!"

Alabaster became jelly as Nathan fell to his knees.

"Hands open and up! Now!" Agent Artois yelled, although he was now only a few feet from Nathan.

Nathan's hands went up and Agent Greene expertly moved them behind his back and placed handcuffs on him.

Oliver was reminded of his rescue and Jimmy's arrest. He barely heard them read Nathan his rights as they walked him away. "Is it over?" he wondered aloud.

A smart looking woman wearing an FBI jacket answered him. "No. They're going to take your statement. You also might have to testify in court. You're lucky this went well. Agent Greene was not happy that you didn't stick to the plan. You should have heard him yelling in the van." She shook her head "How could you do that? You either have more cojones than anyone I've ever met or else you're dumber and luckier than anyone I've ever met."

Oliver knew she didn't truly want an

answer to her question. "Maybe it's all three. What is cojones, by the way?"

The agent laughed and whistled. "I guess you are really lucky, but I think it might be the cojones." She walked away. "Stay here, I'll be back with some paperwork."

Oliver still had no idea what she meant. He sat back in relief. It wasn't dumb luck; it was divine intervention.

Three hours later Agent Greene paced back and forth in Cumberland's library. "You can't just go off script like that! What if he had gotten away? What if he hadn't been an idiot and confessed to everything on tape? You could have ruined everything! And it's your money he would have taken! I could charge you with obstruction for nearly ruining this investigation!"

"But it didn't turn out that way," Oliver said calmly. "I couldn't lie anymore. He underestimated me and overestimated himself." He watched the agent slow his pace. "I should have told you I was going to come clean with him. I apologize. It did turn out okay. You have him in custody. I am going to testify, and Jimmy and the other men are going to testify. And I am praying he will confess. He is as good as convicted."

Greene finally stopped and sat down. "Oliver, I like you. You are astounding. Your faith in people caused Jimmy Ferguson to turn himself in. You had so many people all trying to rescue you, and it was your actions that saved you."

"No," said Oliver. "It was God. It was all God. I still trust Him to take care of all this."

"I have to know that when the time comes you will testify against Westley."

"I will. But I haven't given up hope that he'll confess and save you the trouble of a trial."

Greene stood to leave. "I'll keep you updated. Thank you, Mr. Copeland." He reached out and took Oliver's hand, clasped it firmly, and gave it a hearty shake. "It is an honor to know you."

9

Oliver sat in a leather wingback chair at the Prestige Men's Club, with Simon by his side in a nearly identical one. "I was terrified to tell Nathan I knew the truth. I had no idea what would happen. I was certain he was going to shoot me and walk away."

Simon leaned closer, enthralled by the story. "I can't imagine! I'm not sure I would have been courageous enough, especially knowing that he had given orders to kill you when he abducted you. What happened?"

"He was so demeaned by it that he practically vomited everything he had done. He was bragging about it. I think he's going to have a hard time explaining everything he said on tape. He thinks so much of himself, though, that he's just going to send himself to jail." Oliver took a long drink from his lemonade.

Simon chuckled. "Give him enough rope and he'll hang himself."

Oliver was appalled. "I don't want him to kill himself! My goodness!"

"No, it means he'll take what freedom he thinks he has and talk himself into a guilty verdict." There was no patronization in Simon's reply.

Oliver nodded as he appreciated the meaning of the phrase. "Ah! Yes, he will. By the way, that reminds me. Someone told me I had um…cojones. What does that mean?"

A huge smile bloomed across Simon's face. "It's Spanish. It means you have a lot of courage."

"I've been told I'm courageous quite a few times recently. I don't feel so brave. I am in love with Lucy, but I'm not sure I can tell her. Every time I try to say it, my mouth turns into the Sahara."

"Big brother, you survived being beaten, mugged, and kidnapped. You can't say you're afraid of a kind woman like Lucy."

"I thought I loved Kelly. I thought she was good. I told her I loved her and lost every bit of leverage I had. She beat me! What if…?"

"Stop right there! Lucy is not Kelly. You're not the same man you were when you were with her. You can't let the fear of being hurt stop you from experiencing the joy of love. Who says you need leverage? You faced thugs bent on killing you, and not only survived but overcame. You have the heart of a lion. Share it with someone outside the family." Simon put his glass down so hard the sound of it startled the men at a nearby cluster of chairs.

That made sense to Oliver. "I already survived a broken heart. What could I possibly fear now? Lucy loves me; I'm sure of it. She has said it, but even if she hadn't, I'd know." The "Ode to Joy" streamed through his mind and heart. The prison door swung wide and Oliver wondered if he could fly out of the cage door.

"Listen, Lionheart, I have to go. I have a meeting with the foundation board."

"I'm leaving, too," said Oliver as he stood. "I want to spend some time with Sarah this afternoon."

"Not so fast, big brother. You have a meeting with Langley in ten minutes."

"Oh, yes. Yes," Oliver said. "Right, okay, where's Marcus? He should be here by now."

On cue, Marcus entered, following the waitress to Oliver and Simon.

"Hello, Marcus." Simon stood and shook the assistant's hand, then turned to Oliver. "Thanks for the drinks, Ollie. I will see you later."

10

Nathan could hardly believe his own senses. He sat on one side of the jail's visitation room Plexiglas with that nitwit Oliver on the other. Copeland had actually come to visit. Was he that much of a chump? Only curiosity had moved Nathan to accept the visit. He was long trained in pretending to care, faking emotions, and knowing which ones would work in any situation. Now he decided that Oliver would expect him to be either apologetic or indignant. He went with indignant since it was closer to the truth. He did not plan on further implicating himself in any crimes. "What do you want?" he yelled.

"Voices down! Calm down or you can go back to your cell." Nathan couldn't tell which of the dimwitted guards had issued the warning.

Oliver leaned forward and swallowed, indicating to Nathan that he was nervous. "I wanted to come see you, make sure you're okay, and…" He paused and swallowed again. "See if you wanted to talk about what you did."

"And what is it I did?" Nathan decided to change gears. He leaned back and shook his head to give Oliver the message that he felt sorry for him. "I know you imagine I did all these big bad things. I was your friend and you accused me of some crazy stuff. What is it? I arranged a kidnapping and somehow made sure you would get drunk and get mugged? That's a good one, Oliver." He leaned forward, feigning sadness. "You are confused. I would never have hurt you like that. You muddled the things that happened to you and tried to make rhyme and reason of it. You are wrong. I'm sorry, but I'm not the bad guy. You are… well…you're mixed up. Your memory is playing tricks on you and I'm an easy target. It's a shame."

Oliver's face showed his hurt feelings for a moment, and then it took on a look of pity which infuriated Nathan. But he had taught himself not to show his contempt for people.

"I just want you to know that I forgive you," Oliver said. "I don't know why you are so broken. I want you to be able to confess and feel the freedom that truth will give you. I want you to know that Jesus loves you and He is waiting to forgive you." Nathan was astonished. Oliver sounded as if he actually believed himself!

Nathan wanted so badly to break character and scream, "What a load of crap!" However, he didn't even allow his mind to think it. Instead he made a sad smile. "Poor Oliver. I should be the one to forgive you. It's just sad. Why didn't I ever see how lost you were before? You are very good at pretending you know what's going on around you. I had heard you were brain damaged, but I never believed it." He paused to shake his head as if he felt sorry for Oliver. "Do you see a psychiatrist? Maybe you should."

Nathan could tell from the tightness of Oliver's face that his words had hit home. He watched the man take a deep breath as his lips moved silently, then Oliver said, "I haven't given up hope for you yet. I pray for you every single day."

Now Nathan did feel indignant. God was a prop, and Nathan of all people didn't require the help of some sky-wizard. He did not need or want prayer. His discipline kept him from letting his outrage show. He stood. "Evidently, you can't or won't understand that you are misguided. I just can't watch you do this to yourself or to me." He walked to the door and waited for the stupid guard to let him go through it. He never looked back at the idiot in the visitation room.

As soon as a phone was available, Nathan made a call.

"This is Nick," the deep voice said curtly.

"I'd like you to check up on a friend for me. He needs someone to meet his needs. Give him a full care package from Westley."

"You got it. What's the name and where should I deliver the package?"

"Oliver Copeland. Belle Cay, Connecticut. He has seats for the Philharmonic, and you can bring the package to him there."

"Send payment as usual and then you can consider it done." He hung up the phone.

Satisfied, Nathan returned to the day room to look over who else he could mold to his needs.

11

The concert had been everything Oliver hoped. Now, with the music of Vivaldi still pulsing through his soul, he and Lucy were walking in the park. He knew it was time to tell her how he felt, but fear kept the words inside him. Instead of declaring his undying love for her, he said, "I visited Nathan in jail."

She gripped his hand. "You did? Why?"

"I feel sorry for him. I wanted to tell him I forgive him, and I don't know, I thought he would receive it. I don't think he feels things. I just wonder what could break a man that way."

"Sometimes people are born like that."

Oliver was silent for a moment as he considered Lucy's words. "Well, I think that if he could just know that he is cared for, if he knew that free grace was available, then he could get better. How awful to go through life being so cold, so alone."

"Oliver," she said. "I…" Whatever it was she was going to say went unsaid as her voice trailed off.

A large man walked out of the shadows of the trees that lined the park's path. Even under the lamppost, he remained covered in darkness. A hoodie obscured his face. The only thing Oliver could see clearly was the gun in his hand pointed at Lucy.

In a low timbre, he said, "Give me your wallet! Lady, hand over the purse." He used his gun as a pointing finger to enhance his words.

Maybe the couple waited too long before responding, but it seemed to Oliver that the man did not give them a chance to reply. He used his gun as a fist and hit Oliver's cheek and brow. Then suddenly the huge man had Lucy in his grip, the gun now pointed at Oliver.

Lucy screamed.

"Give me your money!" the large man hissed. Still he didn't give them a chance to respond. His arm moved to Lucy's neck and his other hand raised the gun to point it at

Oliver's head.

"Oliver! Help me!" Lucy choked out. She was crying, her voice muffled from difficulty taking in air.

Oliver didn't waste a moment thinking. "No!" came out as one long scream. No one was going to hurt Lucy. He ignored the gun, ducked and lunged toward the man, hitting him with his full weight, sending him off balance and down. He saw the flash of the muzzle and could almost feel the heat of the bullet move past his face.

The two men grappled as Oliver tried to wrest the weapon from the gunman's hands. The larger man loosened his tight grip on the pistol, still holding it with one hand, and punched Oliver hard in the face with the other. The hit gave Oliver the chance to seize the gun and toss it away. He remained on top of the man, who was now punching him with both hands. He struggled to grab the man's hands in his own as he received blow after blow to his face and chest. The man kicked, hard, but Oliver would not give in. He was not a graceful fighter but his tenacity made up for it.

The blaring sirens of the approaching police cars did nothing to alert the men that their fight was nearly over. Lucy had scrambled away and called the police during the brawl. Two shouting policemen rapidly split the men apart and immobilized them in expert fashion. Oliver was once again reminded of his rescue from Nathan Westley's claws. He calmly allowed the police to handcuff him and walk him toward a cruiser.

Two hours later, Lucy and Oliver were finished being interviewed by the police and were walking out of the emergency room, having been declared free of serious injuries. Oliver felt a rare peace and joy while strolling hand in hand with the amazing dark-haired beauty. "I saw something tonight, something unexpected."

"What was it?" she asked in her smooth voice. She squeezed his hand gently, a sign of encouragement to continue.

"I saw myself through your eyes."

Lucy smiled, "What did you see? Did you see a man who is deeply loved by me?"

"I saw a man, a hero… no one has ever seen me the way you do. You cried out my name and you were sure I would save you. When I saw myself through your eyes, I saw a man, a strong man, not a man weak or in need. No one sees me the way you do. To most people, I'm fragile, broken, or lacking something."

Lucy stopped walking and the couple stood together beneath the glow of a street lamp in the parking lot. "How could I see you any other way?"

Oliver took both her slender hands into his and peered into her eyes. His heart was open wide, and fear fled in the light of love. "Do you see all of me? I think you do. Do you see a man who loves you more than he thought possible? Do you see a man who can hardly believe that he has the chance to be with someone as exquisite as you?"

Lucy blushed but kept her eyes on his, allowing his gaze to delve into her heart and soul. "I do."

Oliver knew he had nothing to fear from her. "I'm sorry I almost let pride keep me away from you. I'm sorry I was so afraid to open my heart. Thank you for breaking down the prison door and setting me free to be the man you perceive me to be."

Cuthbert had arrived. He stepped out of the car and came around to open the door for them. "Good evening, Mrs. Treadway and Mr. Copeland."

Lucy and Oliver slipped into the car. "Thank you, Cuthbert," said Oliver.

"Thank you," said Lucy. Once settled in

the car she turned her attention back to Oliver. "Thank you, my love, for opening yourself to me, for giving me the chance to love you as I have known I wanted to for a few years now."

Oliver leaned toward her and kissed her smooth lips.

She leaned against him, her head on his chest, closed her eyes and fell asleep, obviously exhausted from the night's events. Her breathing was even and her countenance serene.

Oliver held her securely in his arms and vowed to do everything in his power to love her as she deserved to be loved.

12

Oliver was about halfway along the track and he didn't think he could go another step. It seemed his entire body was screaming at him to stop. But he knew from experience that this was just temporary and he could make it through. He was only running; that was nothing compared to Jesus carrying the cross, beaten, bruised, and near broken. He pictured Jesus' bloody back and imagined the weight of the cross, the sins of the world pressing down on it. Then Oliver was through "the wall," feeling light and fast and free.

Alec cheered Oliver on as he made his way around the Copeland Enterprises track. "You're almost there. Just 10 more feet!"

Oliver crossed the finish line but kept

going. He wanted to get further and do better with each day. Getting back to the gym had been grueling at first, but it had once again become an integral part of his day. Even his limp had improved beyond what he had imagined possible. He knew he would likely never again run a five-minute mile, but running brought him a sort of peace and a special communion with God. He prayed, he listened, and sometimes his mind was just quiet. He had not fallen while running in over a month. Maybe soon he would begin running on the Belle Cay Bike Path.

"Alright! Oliver, you're close to the finish line. You're nearly there."

Oliver looked up to see Alec with a towel and a bottle of water in his hands. This time he ran through the finish and slowed to a walk, taking the towel and water with thanks. He walked a final lap around the track to cool down.

Alec caught up to him and walked beside him. "You did a mile and a quarter in 15 minutes twenty-two seconds. That is the farthest and fastest yet."

"Thanks. You're a great personal trainer. What's next?"

"Nothing today. Tomorrow is the weights cycle before your run."

"Great," said Oliver, wiping his face with the towel. "I'm off to shower before work then."

Alec smiled. "Great job. Make sure you include protein in your breakfast."

Oliver savored the steamy shower and its cascade of hot water over his muscles. He knew he would never appreciate the shower so much if it weren't for the sweaty workout that preceded it. There is no rainbow without a storm and no silver lining without a cloud, he knew. Not that the morning work-outs were storm clouds. He enjoyed them very much, but he enjoyed his shower a little more. The sweat and dirt came off him and poured down the drain as he soaped himself and scrubbed his skin. The cleanness of it all invigorated him, and as he cleaned the traces of sweat away he felt pure inside and out. The exercise took away his worries and weakness, the sweat carried toxins away, the soap cleaned away the dirt, and the hot water melted his aches away. After his shower, he felt like a new man.

Oliver dressed slowly, and just as slowly turned his thoughts to the day ahead. What meetings were scheduled and what work awaited him? However, he also couldn't help thinking about the case. It seemed to be taking ages to go to court. He wanted to be finally over with everything, and he couldn't be as long as he had to wait for the court date.

It was probable that Oliver would have to testify as a witness. He had not wanted to, but had already been informed that he would have no choice either way. When Jacob Armand had been tried, Deborah had been spared the agony of testifying. He hoped the same would happen for him. But she had not been the victim in the case, and he was. He knew it was better to be prepared for the likelihood of testifying than to continue wishing he wouldn't have to. Oliver chose to stop wishing and start preparing.

After he was dressed and eating his breakfast of a spinach and egg white omelet, Oliver opened his computer and began writing out every incident he could remember involving Nathan. With his bank statement open, he recorded when and why he had given the man money each time. What he could not recall now, he would hopefully remember later. He was about to begin recording the events of the Chicago trip when Marcus entered, ready to begin the day. Oliver closed his statement and his notebook, but planned to work on his testimony each day until it was as complete as he could make it.

13

The court room was brightly lit, in contrast to the rich wood and dark colors which decorated it. The fluorescent lights buzzed and tried to take over Oliver's thoughts as he made his way to the witness stand. He could see Nathan sitting at the defense table, watching him with a smug look. Although he wished he didn't have to see Nathan go through a trial, he was repeatedly reminded of his dreams which had insisted to him that the truth would set him free. He knew the truth could also set Nathan free from all the pride that tormented him. The judge was speaking to Oliver, giving him instructions, but his attention was stayed on Nathan. The con man appeared a little thinner and perhaps paler than he had before. Oliver felt sorry for the man, who knew no better than to believe he was above everyone else, a man whose arrogance had separated him from being able to make any real connections. He supposed it must have been a very lonely life to live.

Westley had looked at him as a broken man, but Oliver now realized that it was Westley who was the more broken. What happened or what had been missing in his life that had caused him to live a life of hatred and maleficence? Oliver didn't know, but it didn't stop him from praying for the man.

"Mr. Copeland, do you understand?" The judge's voice interrupted Oliver's reflections.

"Yes, I do." Oliver had heard all of the instructions before, from Robert Song, who had been meticulous in preparing Oliver for his time on the stand.

"Very well," said Judge Oakley. "Mr. Hale, you may begin." The judge nodded toward the assistant district attorney.

The prosecutor asked Oliver question after question; each one had been given to Oliver ahead of time so that his memory would not be excessively challenged. Yet his brain wasn't fully cooperating and he felt as if there were too many times that he had to apologize for his befuddled mind. Hale didn't seem to mind at all, and Oliver knew the man was painting a picture of Oliver as the damaged victim of a cold-hearted criminal. Though Hale was happy with the portrait he painted, Oliver was not so happy. He reminded himself that whatever Hale, the jury, or anyone else thought of him, it did not change who he was.

As Oliver was taken through his tale, he watched Nathan grow harder in his seat behind the defense table. The criminal's smug expression became a condescending smile. He shook his head and even gave out a laugh occasionally as Oliver spoke. Westley's attorney tried to quiet the man, but he was too proud to take the advice.

Oliver was sapped after more than four hours of questioning by Morgan Hale. However, he was not allowed to leave just yet. It was the defense's turn. Leland Proust walked back in forth in front of Oliver as he asked his questions, making Oliver seasick as his eyes followed the man to and fro.

"When you were in the flop house in Chicago, did you ever hear any person say the name Nathan Westley?" Proust asked.

"No, but…"

Proust cut him off. "And did you ever

communicate with any person other than James Ferguson, whom you knew as Jimmy?"

"Once there was someone else in the room."

"Was it Nathan Westley?"

"No. I didn't know who it was at the time." Oliver felt as if he were ruining the prosecution's case.

"Could it have been Frank O'Neil?"

"I found out later that it was him."

Proust stopped pacing and stood as close to the witness stand as he was allowed. "Have you ever heard of Stockholm Syndrome, Mr. Copeland?"

"Objection!" Mr. Hale declared, for what seemed the hundredth time in the last two hours.

"Withdrawn," answered Mr. Proust. "What reason could you have for believing anyone other than James Ferguson and Frank O'Neil were involved?" He didn't wait for a reply. "Maybe you thought they were your friends. Maybe you think everyone is your friend,"

"Objection! Conjecture." Hale said loudly.

Judge Oakley leaned forward. "Mr. Proust, please get to your point."

Proust's smile was nearly as smug as Nathan's. "When you came home from your trip to Chicago, when did you next hear from Mr. Westley?"

Oliver was so tired and the fog in his brain was as thick as pea soup. "I'm sorry. I don't remember."

"Well, then let me remind you of what you said earlier to the ADA. You said you called him and scheduled a meeting with him. Why would you do that if you thought he was a kidnapper? Why would you want to contact a man who you supposedly thought had drugged you and had you beaten? Why would you want to talk to man who purportedly abducted you?"

"I…I…" No words would form either in Oliver's mouth or brain. He was too tired to go on.

Oliver's protective younger brother leaned forward and spoke to Hale in an urgent whisper but received a shaking head in response.

Proust didn't take notice of it and gave a sigh. "You can't come up with a reason? Maybe that is because you're making all this up. Maybe you just can't bring yourself to blame the man who held you, who drugged you every single day, several times a day."

"I... know Jimmy held me... but…" He looked at the judge, about to ask for a recess.

Proust jumped in, "Finally, some honesty from you, Mr. Copeland. Perhaps you are finally going to choose integrity and let go of your vendetta."

Oliver wanted to stop, he was drained of energy, he was exhausted of strength. He could no longer hear what Proust was saying. "Please. I…I am ex…ex…" His brain would not provide the words. "I… am…tired."

It was the judge rather than the prosecutor who spoke. "We will recess until tomorrow morning at ten o'clock." He pounded the gavel and the courtroom full of people stood as he did.

Simon rushed to Oliver, who stood at the witness chair, leaning heavily against the back of it. "Come on, big brother. Let's go home."

14

Spring grew as winter dissolved and nourished the land. The April sun brought hope to the world as it proclaimed that winter was temporary and life existed hidden below the cold ground. Oliver and Simon ate breakfast on the patio of Copeland Gardens and watched Cathy and Misha playing. Denise was already at work in the emergency department.

The trial had continued, and Oliver had not been allowed to attend except when he was on the witness stand. Simon had attended every day to be a presence reminding the jury that there were victims. Now his younger brother was telling him about the final day, the closing arguments, and the jury being sent to deliberate.

"Don't worry," Simon told him, "your cross-examination didn't hurt the case against Westley. Jimmy and Frank both testified against him. I don't think there's any doubt that he's guilty."

"I'm not worried. I couldn't help what happened. The defense lawyer was doing his job. Besides, regardless of what happens, God promised justice. If that justice doesn't happen here and now, it will be later. Wouldn't it be great if Nathan would come to Christ?"

"Yeah, it would be," Simon said. "He's just so arrogant. I'm furious with him all the time. How are you not?"

Oliver gathered his thoughts. "I am angry with him often. The thing is, I have to take hold of that. It hurts me to be so mad. It makes me sick. I want him to be locked up in prison, to know at least a part of what he put me through. Every time I catch myself wishing him ill will, I ask God to help me see him as His child. He's broken and lost and God wants him to be saved. I do too, I want God's will more than mine. If he isn't convicted, life will go on and there will be justice one way or another. Maybe mercy will lead him to the truth. Maybe he'll let Jesus pay for his sins. Maybe prison will lead him to the truth. I don't know, but I pray for God's will, not mine."

Simon sat for a moment in silence. He stood, went to his brother, and placed his hands on Oliver's shoulders in a brotherly hug. "I wish I were half the man you are."

Oliver looked back at Simon and beamed a smile. "Well, you can keep wishing." He reached up and mussed Simon's hair. "You know, you're not so bad yourself."

Oliver's phone rang and the caller ID revealed it was Morgan Hale. "Hello, this is Oliver."

"Oliver, it's Morgan. The jury is back and court is convening in one hour."

"Thank you. We'll be there." He told Simon, "The jury is back." Then he dialed Cuthbert as Simon let the nanny know they would be leaving.

Oliver had expected a crowded court room, but other than the lawyers, Nathan, the judge, jurors, and a few journalists, the room was as empty as it had been throughout the trial. Lucy sat next to him on one side, Simon on the other. The three held hands like children anticipating big and possibly frightening news. Though Oliver knew he had nothing to fear, he felt the suspense of the moment. He only realized he had been holding his breath when the jury foreman answered the judge's question.

"We the jury find the defendant, Nathan Westley, guilty of the charge of kidnapping in the first degree. We find the defendant…"

Oliver was no longer listening. He felt an odd sense of elation and sadness together. The truth had won the day, and this young man would not be able to meet the potential he could have had before he turned to crime. Perhaps Nathan would still become the person God meant him to be. Perhaps he would find Jesus in prison.

Whatever happened, it was out of Oliver's hands. He was free.

15

"Daddy, do you have to go on this trip?" Sarah looked through her father's suitcase, ensuring he had everything he would need. She had labeled his outfits for him, not because she didn't trust Lucy but because she still loved to choose his ensembles.

"My sweet daughter, this is not a trip. It's a honeymoon."

"I know, and I want you to enjoy it. I just can't stop imagining you won't come back. I'm really afraid something terrible will happen to you. Daddy, just honeymoon here," Sarah pleaded.

"Listen, I can't promise you that nothing bad will happen. But you can't live your life in fear. I did it for too long. That's not living; it is merely existing. We have to trust in God, His love of us as the Good Father, the Perfect Son, and the Almighty Spirit make it so that there is no room for fear in our lives. When you trust God, you're not afraid of hearing bad news because you know He's gotten you through everything."

"But daddy, I can't lose you!"

Oliver took Sarah and sat her down on the bed, then knelt down in front of her so that they were face to face. "I will do everything in my power to come home safe to you. I promise you that. There are some things we can't control. But what good does it do you to worry?"

"I don't know. I guess it's not helping." Sarah looked lost to Oliver.

"Right. As a matter of fact, it is making things worse. We should be enjoying this time together, and we should be excited about packing my bags for this trip. We should be enjoying our preparations for the wedding. Instead, you're mourning me while I'm right here in front of you."

Sarah stood up, a brave smile on her face. Her resiliency never ceased to amaze Oliver. "Okay, then. Let's get you packed. We have three hours until the wedding and I have to be at Lucy's in an hour. We have people coming over to do our hair and make-up, and there's going to be a photo shoot. Edwin and Uncle Simon should be here soon." She had resumed going through Oliver's bag, removing some shirts and going to the chest of drawers for different ones. As she placed them with their appropriate pants, she said, "Daddy, I want you to enjoy your honeymoon, and I want you to have as much fun as possible."

"Thank you, sweetheart." Oliver placed his cuff links in a small case. "You, Maya, and Edwin will be flying out to meet us in a week. You'll spend your entire spring break with us. In the meantime, you will help Maya and Edwin move in and get comfortable. The three of you will need to supervise the moving company and ensure all of Lucy's things are taken care of properly."

"Yes, of course, daddy." Sarah looked through the cuff links and watches in Oliver's case and nodded her approval.

"And I have a surprise for you," Oliver continued. "The night before you fly out, there will be a party here. Each of you may invite whomever you like; just keep it under fifty kids. Asher and Deborah will be here to chaperone, and Simon and Denise may come as well. Epsilon is going to play. They'll do a set by the pool. The catering is already arranged."

"Oh, daddy! Thank you!" She stood on the tips of her toes to embrace her father. "I'll have to thank Asher as well. Epsilon is much too big to play a high school party. He's so nice."

"That's my girl. There are certain perks to having a rock star in the family. Let's go have some breakfast before you head over to Lucy's place."

The wedding was exactly what Oliver and Lucy wanted: a simple intimate ceremony at the church. Lucy was resplendent in her pale blue silk floor-length gown with pearls lining the bodice. Maya and Sarah wore matching bridesmaid dresses designed by Sarah. The blue of the dresses was a shade darker than Lucy's. With a heart-shaped top and slightly flared skirt that stopped just above the knees, the girls looked both modern and elegant. Edwin, Simon, and Oliver wore matching tuxedos bought just for the occasion.

There would be no reception, or at least not a reception that would be attended by the bride and groom. They left for Cumberland Manor immediately after the ceremony to change clothes, and then went directly to the airport to take a jet to the south of France.

16

Maya and Sarah lounged on the sun patio of the villa while Edwin toured St. Tropez with a friend he'd met on the flight over. Lucy and Oliver were in the kitchen preparing lunch; more accurately, Oliver watched Lucy prepare lunch. He loved watching her do even the simplest things. She sliced fruits and cheeses for the meal and looked pointedly at her husband.

"This would go twice as quickly if you helped," Lucy smiled, holding out a paring knife for him to take.

Oliver ignored the knife and winked. "Dear, I am no good in the kitchen. I can boil water, but I haven't done that for a few years." He held his hands up as if he couldn't help his ineptitude in the kitchen.

Lucy rolled her eyes, took the knife back, and continued cutting fruits. "At least hand me the loaf of bread, please."

"That I can do." He took the long loaf from the hanging basket and put it on the counter, then carried the tray of plates, cutlery, butter, and napkins outside to the table.

The girls stirred from their sunbathing. "Do you want us to set the table, Oliver?" Maya offered.

"No, thank you. But you two may want to go wash up and then see if there is anything else to bring out." Oliver made the table settings ready, then headed back inside to bring the food to the patio.

"This looks almost too good to eat, but I am hungry as a horse!" Oliver took a sliced sweet pepper from the platter and popped it into his mouth. "Delightful!" He carried the food-laden dish to the patio while Lucy toted a pitcher of fruit juice and a bottle of sparkling water.

"Edwin texted me. He and Jean are eating out and he promises to be back by dark. I told him he'll miss out on the bonfire if he isn't." Lucy placed the drinks on the table and took a seat.

Sarah and Maya joined the family at the table, a worried scowl on Sarah's face. "What if Jean isn't the nice young man he pretends to be? What if he is out to get our money? I think you should call Edwin, Daddy, and tell him to come back now."

"Sarah, how hard would life be if you didn't trust anyone?" Oliver poured some sparkling water into Sarah's glass.

"You trusted that horrible Nathan Westley man, and look what happened!" She stomped her foot even as she remained sitting. "It is better never to trust anyone."

"Sweetie," said Oliver, "I wasn't kidnapped because I trusted Nathan. I was kidnapped because he chose to do some very evil things. I choose to trust because although people are not trustworthy all the time, I can always trust God. What happened with Nathan was very frightening, but God did keep me safe, didn't he?" Sarah didn't answer, and Oliver leaned in closer. "Didn't he?"

Sarah forced herself to nod.

Lucy leaned over and hugged her stepdaughter. "You trust me, and I know you trust Maya and Edwin. What relationships will you miss out on if you never trust anyone?"

Sarah took a long drink from her water. "I am happy with the people in my life now. I don't need anyone new." She pulled out her phone. "I'm going to check on Edwin."

Maya gently lowered the phone. "He will hate you if thinks you're treating him like a baby! He's a big boy, and God can take care of him. Now, sister, eat your lunch."

Sarah reluctantly put the phone away and ate, but the look of worry never left her face.

17

Nathan walked into the prison yard and searched the crowd for weaker men he might conform to his needs. He looked at body language and groupings that would tell him the men wanted a leader, a friend, or someone to look up to. There were many men there searching for someone to notice them and be the mother or father in their lives, and it was up to him to find them, to figure out who or what was missing, and to become that for them. Once he did, they would be his toadies, willing to do anything and everything for him. He would have his power back even if it took a little time. It was best to work it one man at a time for now.

He spotted the chump he would start with.

The solitary man was chubby, with charcoal black hair, wearing a uniform just a little too tight for him and walking the perimeter of the yard. Nathan headed toward him, taking note of the way he played with an absent ring on his left hand, how he mouthed words and moved his head in an animated conversation he was not having, and how seemed to be on the losing side of an argument with the imagined other person.

Before he could arrive, his attention was pulled away from Chubs by a brick wall wearing a gray prison uniform stepping into his path. "Where are you going?" came a deep voice from a foot above his own head.

Nathan paused for a moment before looking up and then down, trying to catalogue what he could about the behemoth. The guy was confident in his size and strength, but Nathan thought he was not so sure of his intelligence or identity. He threw his weight around because he didn't trust himself as a person. Nathan, on the other hand, had complete trust in his intellect and acumen. "Oh, hello!" he said. "I'm sorry, I didn't see you. I'm Nathan, and I'm new here. I'm kind of looking for a place to fit in, you know?"

The giant's head blocked the sun and enabled Nathan to see that the angry look on his face did not so much as twitch in response to the stroking of his ego. "I don't care who you are. You think you can walk through my space and get away with it?" His giant hand was suddenly around Nathan's throat.

Nathan tried to sound calm and authoritative. "I didn't realize. But now I know. It won't happen again." He hoped his words conveyed the respect and fear he didn't feel.

"Damn right it won't happen again!" The giant let go of his neck.

For a moment Nathan thought he had won a little, and decided that the giant could eventually be his to use. But just as abruptly as he had been freed from the man's death grip, he was surrounded by other men, apparently the giant's followers.

"You're about to pay for your sins, weasel," the giant informed him.

Nathan looked around and noted every person who stood far off and alone, each man who watched from a group, and every guard who suddenly was looking anywhere but at the mob who was about to thrash him. He'd been beaten before; he could take it. He could use it. Nathan lifted his fists and invited the pounding to commence. Fists and feet pummeled him. He took the pain of each kick and punch and turned it away, put it in a shelf on a box and saved it for another time when he could use it.

At long last, the guards took their attention away from birds flying overhead, untied shoes, or dirty fingernails, and broke the pack off him. At last all the attackers were pushed off of him, and only the guards stood over him. "Everyone back to your cells! Play time is over for today, girls!" The prisoners obeyed casually, as if stopping the fight and returning inside were their ideas.

"Get up!" ordered one of the lazy wannabe cops. "You're fine."

Nathan breathed relief that it was over. He stood slowly and inventoried his bruises to ensure that he really was okay. He decided he was, but said, "I need to go to the infirmary."

"Do ya, Mary? Do you need the nursie to kiss your bruises?" The guard pushed him toward the door. "Go on, then."

The next day, Nathan wore his bruises and bandages like trophies, circumventing the center of the yard and heading toward Chubs along the edge of the fence. He didn't have a chance to open his mouth.

A string of cuss words flew from the dark man's mouth. "Stay away from me, loser."

"Sorry, man. It's just, I could use a friend. I'm willing to pay for your friendship, dude." He tried appealing to the man's pride, to appear in need of his protection. "I'm alone here."

"I'm not your friend, or dude, or buddy. We are all alone, and I don't give a crap about you. Protect yourself, jerk." The man stopped walking. "Find someone else to be your friend, cause it ain't gonna be me."

Nathan walked away, this time to a man he had noticed sitting at a table ignoring yesterday's fight. When he approached, the wiry man glared at him, then turned and buried his face into a book.

Nathan sat down beside him. "Hey, I've read that book! Yeah, it was great."

The man sighed in frustration. "Do I care what you think of some book? Get lost. You got nothing to offer me or anyone else here. Just do your time and let me do mine. If you want companionship, join a gang, kiss up to one of the blockheads, or let the queers know you're available. Whatever you do, stop harassing me." He pointedly reopened the book and read it as if Nathan were not sitting next to him.

Looking around, Nathan decided to join in the basketball game being played by half a dozen men. He approached the group and waited for the ball to go out of bounds. When it did, he caught it and tossed it back to the group. Instead of gratitude or an invite to play, he got a short sentence made long by only expletives used as adjectives, adverbs, and punctuation which queried what he thought he was doing and who did he think he was doing it.

None of the six men bothered to wait for an answer. Instead he was once again met with a flurry of furious fists. This time, when the fight was broken up, he was lifted to his feet. Manacles were put on his feet and hands and he was dragged to a small cell and shoved inside.

Nathan was in solitary confinement. "What the…?" He tried to ask the question but was not allowed to finish.

"Shut up. You're in solitary for the next two days. You can't keep fighting with everyone. If you can't handle general population then your stay here will be reevaluated.

"But, I didn't…"

Once again, he was not allowed to finish his statement. "You didn't do anything? There have been two fights in the last two days, and you were at the center of both of them. You.

Now sit down on the bench, inmate." His calm demeanor irked Nathan for reasons he could not pinpoint. It was as if Nathan did not matter, and nothing he said or did had any significance to the guard.

Nathan obeyed, and the chains were removed. The guard left and swung the heavy door closed behind him. Nathan was alone with his thoughts, his future, and his past.

18

Once a month, Oliver traveled to Danbury to visit Nathan in prison. Westley had held on to the secret of his true identity, so Oliver had no choice but to call him by the name he had given the prison system as his own. The man always refused to see him, but Oliver refused to give up. Simon had suggested that the man would never be willing to hear the Gospel, much less accept Christ, but Oliver had seen God do the impossible. So he waited, even as he expected the guard to call his name and let him know that, once again, Nathan had refused to see him. This week it seemed to be taking longer, and his hopes were lifted. Maybe this was the breakthrough day when his kidnapper would agree to see him and begin a dialogue.

His time might be better spent going to visit Jimmy and mentor him through his new Christian walk, but Oliver couldn't bring himself to give up on Nathan. So, for now, he would continue exchanging letters with Jimmy. The letters were exciting; he could see the growth in the man who was so hungry for the kingdom of God. Jimmy asked insightful questions, which often had Oliver searching the Scriptures for the right answer. He answered queries from Oliver with perceptiveness and passion. Jimmy said that although he was dreadfully sorry for what he had done, getting arrested was the best thing that had ever happened to him, as it had resulted in his salvation. Oliver considered what his next letter to Jimmy might include, eventually deciding that he would suggest they read Philippians and discuss a few questions that Oliver would provide. Even preparing the lessons for Jimmy had helped Oliver grow into a deeper relationship with God. That was one reason he wanted to see Nathan so badly. He needed Westley to understand that he truly forgave him and hoped he could share the Gospel with him.

The guard entered the room and called a short list of names, the people who would follow him into the visitation room. "Carla Hornbeck, Justin Combes, Oliver Copeland, and Tiana Washington, please follow me." He waited for the four people to join him.

Oliver almost didn't get up; he was used to being called alone and being told to leave. It took a moment to grasp that he was about to visit Nathan. His heart beat out Bach's *Toccata* with nervous anticipation, but hope made him jump up. He collected himself and joined the others by the door. What would he say? Why had Westley finally agreed to see him? He breathed a prayer and felt the peace of God fill Him. *I will give you the words; you only have to be willing.*

Oliver followed the guard into a small bright white hallway with several gray doors. Two more guards stood at a table; one searched him, though he had already been searched. "Please remember, you may not touch the inmates except to greet them or say good-bye. Any gifts other than hygiene items must be handed over to the guards and will be distributed at a later time. Sit down on your side of the table. If you have brought items for the inmate, set them in the middle of the table. Do not hand them directly to the inmate. If a guard asks something of you, it is for your safety. Please listen and obey immediately. If a guard gives an order to an inmate, please do not interfere; just wait for the inmate to comply. Do you understand?"

Each of the people said a quick yes; all but Oliver had heard this speech numerous times before. Filled with calm and hope, Oliver followed the first guard through a door to the left and into a large room. There were no decorations, no extras, just slate blue walls and one-piece tables with attached benches. There was nothing to upset an inmate and nothing for him to throw or otherwise use as a weapon. It was stark. Was prison life this bare?

Oliver scanned the people in the room. Most of the tables had a man on one side in his prison white or grey and another person on the opposite side, softly talking. One woman cried as she spoke to a man much younger than herself, perhaps her son. At another table a man in the prison grey pants and shirt was laughing, quietly speaking to a woman and child. Oliver scanned the room and found Westley sitting, his white pants and shirt done up neatly, his hair combed back. He might have looked sharp except for the bruises and welts covering his face.

Sitting down on his side of the table, Oliver could see just how fresh the injuries were. There was dried blood over Nathan's right eyebrow, an open cut on an egg-sized bump under his left eye, and a deep purple bruise on his left jaw. He had been beaten, and it had clearly been at the hands of more than one person. Even so, beneath the black and blue face, his steel eyes revealed his supercilious nature.

Oliver nodded a greeting. "I suppose it's futile to ask how you're doing. What happened?"

"What do you think happened? You sent me to prison and I got beat up!" As he began to raise his voice, a guard approached, and Nathan lowered his voice. "But I'm fine. I won't be broken, and when they find out you're a lying imbecile, they'll let me out. I'll sue you and maybe you'll enjoy the perks of prison."

Oliver let the pitiful man vent and chose not to answer.

"Why are you here, anyway? Why do you keep coming? I don't want to talk to you. I don't want to hear you tell me how much Jesus loves me."

"But you agreed to see me today. Why is that?"

"Maybe it'll take me telling you to your face that I do not want to be your friend, your buddy, or your disciple. You're pathetic."

"I don't want to be friends with you. I want to tell you that I forgive you, and I hope you will let that forgiveness let you move forward with your life." Oliver paused and was about to continue when Nathan cut in. He supposed the man didn't like pauses in conversation, or maybe he was more interested in speaking than listening.

"Who are you to forgive me? You're ridiculous, you know. You think you're so good? You aren't."

"I'm no one special. I know it doesn't matter to you that I no longer hold any bitterness toward you. But I needed this for me. I am free from your prison. You can be free from yours too. Not this physical one, but the mental one you've constructed."

Nathan laughed, and the sound was like acid spilling out and burning his own heart away. "Now you're a hippie? I'm in a mental prison? This prison is real, and I'm here because of you! I was beaten because you falsely accused me. It may as well have been you who hit and kicked me!"

He had gotten loud again and this time the guard put his hand on Nathan's shoulder to quiet him. "One more time and your visit is over."

Nathan acted as if the guard had not intervened, but when he spoke again he was more composed. "Forgive me all you want. I do not forgive you. I feel sorry for you."

"It makes no sense to feel sorry for a person who has found joy and freedom, does it? You are so broken, so alone. I wish you would just open your heart a little and accept how deeply God loves you. You told me about the terrible things you've done. God wants to forgive you. Are you sorry for any of it?" Oliver had no trouble finding words or phrases. The language flowed from him without a stutter or pause, as if he were reading it from a screen. "I've done wrong as well. Everyone has. There is not a single person other than Jesus who lived a perfect life. You can take all of those failures to God, ask for forgiveness, make Jesus your Lord, and believe He is Christ, raised from the dead for your life."

Nathan was looking at the table as Oliver spoke but looked up when he paused. "Look, if there is a God, why would he care so much about forgiving people who have done horrible stuff? If it were me, I'd just burn them all."

Oliver was encouraged. "It does sound too good to be true, but it is true. It is that simple."

This time when he finished speaking, Nathan remained silent, but placed a hand on the tender bruises of his face.

"How were you beaten? Weren't the guards watching?" Oliver was concerned. He could see how badly the injuries must hurt, and he could remember the pain after he had been beaten.

"I guess someone thought I needed to learn a lesson. He thought I was too high and mighty for him. I suppose the guards agreed. They looked the other way until I was taken to the hospital wing." Once again Westley absently touched his swollen face. "Like I said, they won't break me." He didn't sound convinced by his own words.

"That sounds like a terrible way to learn a lesson."

"Whatever," said Nathan, as he lowered his hands and sat up straighter in his chair. "I told you I'm not interested in hearing this crap from you."

"No profanity!" said a nearby guard with authority that made Oliver sit up straighter himself.

"I hope you choose to deal with yourself and let God deal with you. You are in here a long time, and there isn't anyone else knocking on the door." Oliver sat forward. "I don't need your forgiveness. Jesus forgave me, and He wants to forgive you too. Be blessed. I mean it. I mean everything I said."

"Just go."

"If you change your mind, or if you need anything, let me know." Standing, Oliver walked to the exit to be let out. As he followed the guard to the door, he almost looked back once more, but changed his mind. Whatever happened, Oliver had done all he could, and now it was up to the Lord. He felt lighter; the weight of Nathan, his kidnapping, and all that had accompanied it were gone. But then as he was about to go through the door held open by the guard, he heard Nathan's quiet voice.

"Hey, don't go."

He didn't know what he expected, perhaps he assumed Nathan Westley would sit stone-faced, angry, or smug. But Oliver turned back and saw Nathan visibly deflated, head down in his hands. The sight rejuvenated his hope. He returned to the table and sat down, but did not speak.

19

He didn't want Oliver to leave. This man had been genuine. Even after everything he had done to him, he could see the authenticity in him. He could see that he believed everything he said. Oliver couldn't leave him wrecked like this. Two days alone and he had not known who he was anymore. Two days alone and he had been unable to convince himself that he was going to survive prison alone. He had to stop Oliver from leaving because somehow he knew that he wanted to be like Oliver. He wanted what Oliver had, not his money or position, but his contentment, his calm, and his confidence.

"Hey, don't go. "Did he sound desperate? He felt desperate.

Oliver turned around slowly and walked back to the table. If he had been allowed he would have grabbed him and held him. But he sat there thinking about who he was and who he wished he was. Somehow, he knew he had to tell Oliver the truth. What was it Jimmy had said that Oliver kept telling him? "The truth will make you free?" Okay then, he would begin with some truth and it scared him. He was afraid for the first time since he had been Billy.

"My name is William Thompkins. Bill. I am a fraud. I am a liar. I'm ready to be real, Man." He felt such relief. He kept speaking and each word made him feel a little more. He suddenly knew that Oliver meant it when he said that he loved him.

"I believe you do love me. I mean…no one has ever cared about me like you have. No one has ever loved me. What you're saying doesn't make a lot of sense to me, but I think you mean it." He looked up at met Oliver's gaze. "I can tell when people are lying, and I can tell when they mean what they're saying. You believe what you say and somehow I believe it too. It's true. Jesus loves me, too. I have done horrible things to you and to so many people. Could He really forgive me?" Tears streamed down Billy's face. How could he feel so happy and so devastated at the same time? If there was a word for this feeling, he didn't know what it was. "I don't deserve to be forgiven. I deserve to be in this prison! God, I am so sorry! I have done so much worse and so much more than anyone knows." He was full on crying and the guard had stepped close to him, but instead of reprimanding him as he should, allowed him to cry.

Billy was not aware of the other people in the large room. He didn't see or care about the people nearby staring at him. He wanted what it was Oliver had. He wanted this freedom, this forgiveness. But there was so much and when he confessed it as who he really was, he would spend life in prison. He had no idea how to be who Oliver believed he could be. He lifted his head and opened the eyes he had not realized were closed. "How do I do it? How do I become a Christian?" Nathan would never have been able to ask this, but Billy wanted it more than he wanted his next breath.

Oliver was beaming. The smile on his face shone out of his eyes. "You only have to confess, that is say and mean that Jesus is your Lord, the Master of your life, and believe that He is alive, resurrected from His death on the cross for your forgiveness. That's it. Then eternal life is yours. I'll make sure you're hooked up with the prison ministry so they can teach you and help you grow and learn."

"Is it really that simple?" The happiness he felt was something the word happy couldn't cover. Billy wanted to stand up and shout it to everyone in the room, but he wanted to follow the rules so he stayed seated. "Jesus is my Lord! He is alive, isn't He! He is no joke! Oliver, I don't know how to thank you. I tried to have you killed, but you loved me enough to tell me about Jesus. I don't get it. How did you do that?" Bill Thompkins had a smile, the first genuine one of his life, happiness or was this joy filled him and he could not contain it. He cried more freely, unable to stop the flow of tears or squelch his need to laugh.

"I didn't do it. Jesus did." Oliver reached to take Billy's hand but the guard leaned closer and he stopped.

"Thank you, Jesus."

Billy looked at the man across the table and wanted to know everything he could from this man. Nathan Westley had died and Billy Thompkins had been resurrected, no longer a terrified little boy, but free to be a man and experience life.

20

"Daddy, why do you insist on doing dangerous things? Do you know what could have happened to you? Please, promise me you won't keep going to that prison to see that vile man. What if there had been a riot, or worse?" Sarah stood in the doorway of Cumberland, hands on her hips and red-faced.

"Sweetheart, please let me in. I'm so tired. Let's go into the library and talk by the fire over some hot chocolate."

Sarah stepped aside and let her father enter, then followed him to the library, waiting for her father to be seated before seating herself and speaking. "I'm sorry, daddy. You know I worry about you."

Oliver sighed. "It is my job to worry

about you, daughter dear." He was so tired of going over this with her. He didn't know what more he could say to convince her. "Nothing happened, and if it had, we would have trusted God to take care of us, regardless."

"Daddy, don't you get it? I can't lose you. I need you. You have to take care of yourself." She let a tear roll slowly down her cheek and drop onto her designer blouse.

"I do take care of myself. I'm not out there risking my life. I plan to be here to take care of you, Edwin, Maya, and Lucy for many more decades. What can I do to help you get over this fear?"

"I don't know, daddy."

The library doors opened. Lucy entered carrying a dinner tray, followed by Edwin carrying an urn of hot chocolate and Maya carrying a tray of mugs and marshmallows. Lucy set the tray down by her husband and kissed him gently, settling into the chair next to him "Charlotte figured you would be hungry. I can barely believe he finally let you see him. It is a miracle. It gives me hope that he may eventually give in to God."

"It is so good to come home to my family. Thank you." He ate some soup and it satisfied a hunger he hadn't realized he felt. He collected his thoughts. "You'll never believe what happened today! I don't know which part to tell you first. Nathan told me his real name." Oliver reached into his pocket. "I wrote it down in case I forgot it. William Thompkins. His name is Bill."

"What?" Lucy jumped from her chair and sat on the arm of Oliver's. "Wow, how did that come about? It really was a day of miracles at Danbury."

"It came about because, somehow, something got through. He had been beaten fairly badly."

Sarah interrupted, "You see! You should not be going to that horrible place, daddy."

"Sarah, I am fine. Now let me tell this."

"Yes, sir," she said bowing her head.

"That beating did something. It broke through something in him. He actually admitted to all the wrong he had done, he apologized and he asked how to become a Christian!"

"What?" Lucy exclaimed breathlessly.

Oliver answered again in case she had not heard, realizing after he started speaking the phrase had not been a question but an exclamation. "He asked for forgiveness and let me share the Gospel with him. It was absolutely amazing."

Edwin spoke up from his place on the

floor, "Honestly, Oliver, I didn't really think he would ever accept Jesus. I thought you were wasting your time. I would've given up on him. He did such awful things."

"How could I not forgive him for what he did? Am I perfect? Far from it. I couldn't give up on him if Jesus wouldn't."

"You are a good man, Oliver." Edwin added a heap of marshmallows to his steaming mug. "I know my father would be happy to think you are my stepdad."

"Yes, but daddy, being so kind to people is going to get you hurt. It nearly got you killed!" Sarah moved to sit at Oliver's feet.

Maya sat next to Sarah on the floor. "Sarah, you're going to get hurt in life even if you're playing it as safe as possible. Oliver and Mommy got attacked in the park while walking along and minding their own business. Besides, Oliver is not selfish, nor could he be. If he was, well, he wouldn't be the man he is. He's strong, and he is capable of more than you give him credit for. Don't forget he fought off that armed robber with his bare hands."

Oliver sat a bit taller in his seat and his vision blurred with tears held back.

Maya continued, "He walked into a prison and faced a man who hated him. He fought off a thug and he took in my mom, brother, and me. I'd say your dad, our dad, is one man you don't ever have to worry about."

Lucy poured a cup of hot chocolate for Oliver, brought it to him, and sat on his lap. Ignoring Maya's groan, she hugged the man she loved. "Well, I think we ought to change the subject. Your head may get too big if we keep this up." Turning her attention to the kids, she said, "There's a party next week in New Haven to raise money for Born Free America, and I believe you all could use new outfits to attend. Shall we go shopping tomorrow?"

Oliver and Edwin suppressed the moans they wanted to release, neither wanting to voice his distaste for shopping while the girls eagerly agreed to a day of picking out clothes, accessories, and shoes. Soon Oliver was watching his family plan for the upcoming fundraiser.

21

Acrobats in brightly painted bodysuits did nearly unthinkable feats above the heads of the party-goers. Music wafted from hidden speakers as dancers in gossamer skirts and pale leotards moved their bodies in unison to the rhythm. Video stations around the room played short documentaries about animal cruelty and circuses. Oliver checked his watch for the tenth time in the last hour. He had agreed to stay at the party until ten, and saw that ten long minutes remained. The party was excellent; even he was enjoying it. The cause was a good one, and he had seen evidence that the money being raised was substantial. But the lights, sound, crowd, and activity were getting to him; he was ready to leave and enjoy the quiet of Cumberland Manor. He retreated to the Copelands' corner table and read a pamphlet about animal rehabilitation.

The table was empty. His family were all enjoying the event. Lucy had been chatting with various socialites, Maya was dancing, and Edwin was watching one of the performers in her intricate routine. Oliver had last seen Deborah and Ash at a video station asking questions to a Born Free America representative. Simon and Denise were making the rounds with friends. He was unsure where Sarah was; she had been by his side for most of the evening, but now he didn't see her. Having finished reading every word of the pamphlet, Oliver checked his watch again, six more minutes. Maybe, if he took his time, he could begin heading out now. He looked around the venue to locate Lucy and moaned when he caught sight of her. She was talking to Vera and Felix.

Was engaging with Vera in conversation worth the chance to leave the party? The woman would want to talk for another hour. Oliver hated the idea of being rude to her. Oliver chose the third option, the chicken's way out. He headed to the coat check and decided to wait outside. He would call Lucy and let her know he was waiting after he called Cuthbert for the car.

Sarah had stepped outside to call Jackson, since she had promised him a party update before his bedtime. Both he and Kyle thought they should be able to attend the shindig, but they were not old enough for the event. She had appeased her disappointed cousin by promising to call him. He was supposed to be in bed nearly an hour earlier, but time had gotten away from her and she knew Jackson would still be awake, probably playing some video game and waiting for the promised call.

She was about to hit dial when Walker Forsythe appeared. The tall handsome boy from her class had a reputation for being a ladies' man. The captain of the tennis team had been trying to dance with her all evening, and up to now she had managed to avoid him.

"Hi, darling," he said, flipping his long curly locks.

Sarah had no patience for people who called her darling, honey, or sweetheart when they had no right to. "Walker, I was about to make a phone call. I'll talk to you Monday at school."

"I want to talk to you now, though." He

closed in on her, just inches away.

With each of his forward steps she stepped back until her back was against the brick wall of the hotel. "Please, back up."

He stepped closer. His breath smelled of cheese. "Don't worry, sugar, no one will see us. You look so beautiful tonight. You deserve to be with the most eligible and best looking bachelor at Belle Cay Prep. You win the prize, honey."

Sarah was outraged, "I'm not a piece of candy! I'm going inside now, please let me by."

He pushed his weight against her, "You know that's not what you want. Give me a kiss." He leaned down and pressed his lips to hers.

Sarah pressed her own lips tight together and turned her face away.

Walker's hand gripped her face hard and turned it back to his. He squeezed, trying to open her mouth. His face was an inch away, waiting to stick his stinking tongue into her mouth.

Suddenly, Walker's weight was lifted off her. "Stop! Leave my daughter alone!" Oliver's voice was like an angel's trumpet in Sarah's ears.

It was only then Sarah realized she had

shut her eyes, readying herself for the attack she thought was guaranteed. She blinked to see her father holding Walker's jacket and leading him back to the sidewalk.

"Never touch my daughter again," he said. "If I ever even think you have touched her or any young woman again, I will report you to the authorities. Do I need to ask you again to stay away from my girls?"

"No, no sir!" Walker began to do a half-run back inside.

"Mr. Forsythe," said her father. "You have something to say."

"Yes, sir. I am sorry."

"Not to me!" Oliver looked larger and more imposing than Sarah had ever seen him.

Walker turned back and walked slowly up to Sarah. "Sarah, I am so sorry. Please forgive my presumption. It will never happen again." He barely looked at her and rushed back into the party.

Sarah shivered and Oliver put his jacket around her bare shoulders. He took her hand in his and they walked together back to the party. She wondered when it was that her daddy had become a superhero, and how had she not noticed his strength before that night.

22

Oliver lifted his face up and let the warm sun energize him. The forest teemed with life, and the sound of it was as exhilarating as the beauty of the trees, flora, and fauna surrounding him. Asha walked beside him, her tiny hand in his. She asked question after question, and he wondered if there was something within little girls that gave them an endless stream of words. When she didn't have a question, she had a story, and when the story might end, there was another one to follow. His heart fairly burst for her.

Lucy walked beside him, her camera at the ready. Oliver guessed she might have taken a hundred pictures so far and there was about another hour left on the hike. "Oh, darling!

Look at that bird! What kind is it?" She lifted her camera and snapped a photo as a woodpecker flew from the side of a tree to somewhere further from the bother of people in his woods.

Asher and Deborah were behind them, little Daniel toddling beside his patient parents. Asher carried him at times, but let his son walk as much as he liked. They had fallen about twenty feet behind, so Oliver stopped and pointed out a fascinating tree to Asha. She immediately let go of his hand and went to explore the large squat tree in an area where the rest of the trees were tall. The trees all seemed to be reaching for heaven, each trying to outdo the others with how close they could get their branches to the sky. But this tree had grown out rather than up, its trunk and branches acting as a playground for the people who might come across it.

"Where are the kids?" asked Asher as they caught up to Lucy and Oliver.

"Ah, they think they're too old to come along on a family hike. You know Sarah and Maya always have plans. It takes something more than a walk in the woods to get them away from their social lives. Edwin is doing a project for school."

"I have to say, as much as I love Sarah, it

is nice to see her finally letting you out of her sight," Deborah said as she helped Daniel climb onto the lowest branch of the tree. "How is she doing?"

"That attack should have traumatized her, but it seems like it had the opposite effect. She is more confident now, seems more secure, and has become her old self again. I am still insisting on counseling anyway. She's seeing Pastor Kennedy once a week." Oliver took his backpack off and pulled out several water bottles, passing them around to all the adults. He checked both children's cups and refilled Asha's.

Lucy snapped photos of the children and Deborah as they played on the tree until Asher plucked Daniel off the branch where he was climbing and put him on his back.

"It's time to go, kids." He bent down and kissed Deborah, causing the baby to giggle and Asha to beg for one more minute.

"No more minutes, little girl. Let's go." Asher began to walk away, knowing his daughter would follow.

She looked toward Oliver in hopes that he wouldn't be able to resist her. "Honey, pleeeeease! Just one more minute."

He scooped the child up in his arms. "You heard daddy. Besides, I'm hungry as a horse and I could eat a bear! Let's finish our hike so we can go get something good to eat!" He tickled her ribs, and she giggled and pressed in tight against him.

There is nothing so invigorating as the exhaustion that comes from something like a good walk in the company of people you love, Oliver thought to himself. The fresh air, the sun, the forest, and the life around him revitalized him. His family restored him. He felt there was nothing he couldn't do with them at his side. Finally, his soul was unbound. He put Asha on his shoulders and opened his arms wide, lifted his face up and breathed in his freedom.

ABOUT THE AUTHOR

Donna is an ordained minister, author, blogger, and preschool administrator living in Ocoee, Florida. She remains active as she works toward a master's degree in Christian counseling, writing the daily devotional blog Salt & Light and serving God through street and prayer ministries with I-Drive Church in Orlando, Florida's tourist district. She has written several Bible devotionals, three novels, a novella, and compiled a cookbook.

You can read her blogs at www.DonnaLCampbell.com

Follow Donna on Facebook at www.facebook.com/DonnaCampbellBooks and www.facebook.com/SaltnLightBibleBlog

Printed in Great Britain
by Amazon